Biggie
and the
Devil
Diet

Biggie
and the
Devil
Diet

Nancy Bell

THOMAS DUNNE BOOKS / St. Martin's Minotaur New York

THOMAS DUNNE BOOKS.
An imprint of St. Martin's Press.

BIGGIE AND THE DEVIL DIET. Copyright © 2002 by Nancy Bell. All
rights reserved. Printed in the United States of America. No part of
this book may be used or reproduced in any manner whatsoever
without written permission except in the case of brief quotations
embodied in critical articles or reviews. For information, address St.
Martin's Press,
175 Fifth Avenue, New York, N.Y. 10010.

www.minotaurbooks.com

Library of Congress Cataloging-in-Publication Data

Bell, Nancy, 1932–
    Biggie and the devil diet: a mystery / Nancy bell.—1st ed.
        p. cm.
    ISBN 0-312-30184-7
    1. Biggie   (Fictitious   character: Bell)—Fiction.   2. Women
detectives—Texas—Fiction.   3. Grandmothers—Fiction.   4. Texas—
Fiction.   I. Title.

PS3552.E5219 B49 2002
813'.54—dc21

                                                        2002071274

First Edition: November 2002

10 9 8 7 6 5 4 3 2 1

Biggie
and the
Devil
Diet

Prologue

I see the Angel of Death," Rosebud said, gesturing toward the afternoon sky with one big, black hand. "See her? Up yonder, settin' on a cloud." He pulled a cigar out of his pocket and slowly unwrapped it, then sniffed it, just as casual as could be, for all the world like he'd just made a comment on the weather. "Un-huh."

I looked at the sky, but all I could see was a pair of big thunderheads rising up like soapsuds behind the Muckleroy house.

Willie Mae dropped a just-peeled potato into the pan in her lap. "Humph," she said.

"Funny, I always thought the Angel of Death would be a man." Biggie sat in the swing next to Willie Mae, shelling peas. She nudged the porch floor with her toe to get the swing going. "Was she carrying a scythe, Rosebud?"

Rosebud held a kitchen match to the end of his cigar and puffed hard to keep it lit. "Nuh-uh," he said, "that there's the Grim Reaper. The Angel of Death looks just like any other angel."

"I'll bet you know a story about that, Rosebud." I looked up at him from where I was sitting on the porch steps. Rosebud has a story for just about every occasion.

Rosebud didn't answer. He was blowing smoke rings and watching them disappear in the slight breeze that rustled the leaves of the big pecan tree in front of the house.

I live with my grandmother, Biggie, in a big, white house on the corner of Elm Street and Sweet Gum Lane in Job's Crossing, Texas. Rosebud and Willie Mae live in their own little house in Biggie's backyard. I am thirteen and starting the eighth grade this fall. I have lived with Biggie since I was six. Before that, I lived with my parents in Dallas. My daddy owned his own business renting portable toilets to construction sites. My daddy died, and my mother, who is the nervous type, could not take care of an active child like me, so Biggie came and packed up my things and brought me here to live with her. Rosebud and Willie Mae came to us a year later. Willie Mae is a voodoo lady. Biggie is a very important person in town and is a charter member of the Daughters of the Republic of Texas, James Royce Wooten Chapter.

I sat for a while listening to the "pop-pop" of peas falling into the bowl and the occasional "thunk" of a peeled potato dropping into Willie Mae's pan.

"Biggie," I said, "tell about how Job's Crossing got its name."

2

"My soul, J.R. You've heard that a hundred times." She dropped a handful of pea hulls into the grocery sack at her feet.

"I'd like to hear it again." I know how much Biggie loves that story.

"Well, if you insist." She set her bowl on the swing beside her and commenced to speak. "It was back when Mr. Stephen F. Austin decided to bring a colony of settlers to Texas. My people all lived in Tennessee before that time. Your ancestor helped found the city of Knoxville. Did you know that, son?"

I nodded.

"Well." Biggie sat up straight in the swing and put her hands on her knees. Her little-bitty feet hung six inches above the floor. "So, my great-great—well, I can't remember how many 'greats' he was—grandfather, James Royce Wooten, set out from Tennessee to Texas to join Austin's colony down in central Texas. He was a brave man to make that trip alone, doncha know, and many hazards awaited him along the trail, from bandits to bears to hostile Indians."

"Golly," I said, thinking how the story got better every time Biggie told it.

"We Wootens have always had grit." Biggie reached for her glass of iced tea, which stood on the porch rail. She took a sip. "Grandpa James Royce wasn't afraid of man nor beast—but there was one thing he couldn't fight."

"What, Biggie?"

"Disease, that's what. A plague descended on that poor brave man so that he was unable to pursue his dream of joining Mr. Austin and his colony. But true to the Wooten character, when handed a lemon, my great-great—whatever—grandfather made lemonade."

"What kind of disease, Biggie?" I knew, but I also knew she wanted me to ask.

"Boils," Biggie said. "James Royce Wooten came down with a bad case of boils. You don't see that much in modern times, but back in the old days it wasn't an uncommon disease at all. Naturally, James Royce knew what to do. He doctored himself with slabs of salt bacon to draw the poison out, but, still, they bothered him quite a lot. Once one boil would heal up, two more would appear on another part of his body. Still, James Royce forged on, determined to reach the center of Texas." She stuck her fingers down to the bottom of her now-empty tea glass and pulled out a piece of ice. She plopped it into her mouth and chewed thoughtfully before continuing. "And he would have, too, except for the fact that somewhere around Fort Smith, Arkansas, a big red boil popped up on his, um, his rear end, doncha know."

I nodded.

"Well, seeing as how Grandpa James Royce was traveling on horseback and leading a supply wagon pulled by two oxen, he was becoming more than a little uncomfortable on the trail."

"I bet!" I said.

"He decided to cross over into Indian Territory, which is now Oklahoma, and enter Texas by crossing the Red River."

"I bet he was attacked by Indians."

"Nope. He never saw any. But his boil was getting

worse. When he came to the Red River, he found a ferryman to take him across into Texas. He camped there for the night and then set out again traveling due south. About sundown, he came to Wooten Creek—of course, it wasn't called that then. Weary and burning with fever from the boils, he decided to make camp there for the night. That evening along about twilight, as he was resting beside his campfire looking around at the tall trees, listening to the sound of the running creek, and thinking about the nice bass he had just fried up for his supper, what should he see but a family of white-tailed deer come out of the woods to stand in the clearing not fifty feet from where he sat. The deer stared at Grandpa just as bold as you please, and Grandpa stared back. Thoughtfully, he dug his bare toe into the fine black loamy soil. It felt rich and cool against his bare skin. It reminded him of his home back in Tennessee. 'Ample game, good soil, and a creek full of fish,' Grandpa thought, 'a feller could live right well in these parts.' Then he thought about how he'd heard central Texas was full of scrub oak and limestone boulders the size of a cow. He pondered how much he hated the thought of getting back on his horse what with his boil paining him so terribly." Biggie frowned like she had the boil herself.

"So that's when he decided to stay here?"

"Not quite," Biggie said. "First, he decided to have a little swim in the creek before bedding down for the night. He swam back and forth across the creek. Once he rolled over on his back and just floated there, watching the moon up in the sky."

"I've done that before."

5

"You bet you have. Well, when Grandpa got out of the creek and was getting back into his clothes, he noticed a funny thing. His boils were all gone—vanished without even a trace of a scar! 'It's a miracle!' he shouted. 'Praise the Lord!' "

"Was it a real miracle?"

"You betcha. Well, right then and there, Grandpa Wooten made up his mind. He wasn't riding another mile. He'd just homestead right here on the banks of Wooten Creek—and here he stayed. The very next day, Grandpa set about building himself a cabin in a grove of pines right near the creek. I guess you know what happened next."

"More people came, and pretty soon they had a town," I said.

"That's about it," Biggie said. "It took awhile, of course. In due course, Grandpa James Royce took a bride, one Eleanor Ann Muckleroy, the prettiest girl in town, which wasn't saying much because at that time there were only three females. One was already married, and the other was sixty-seven years old. James Royce never left Kemp County again except the time he had to go down to San Jacinto and help Gen. Sam Houston beat the tar out of old Santa Ana. After Texas won its independence from Mexico, he built Eleanor Ann a fine house on the hill, where the family graveyard sits now, and they had themselves eight fine strapping boys."

"That's a good story, Biggie. Makes me proud to be a Wooten."

"Me, too," Biggie said, "but a person can't rest on the laurels of those who came before him. We must all make our own mark in the world. Always remember that."

"Yes'm." I hoped she wasn't going to give me one of her lectures on the responsibilities of being a Wooten and living up to the family name.

I breathed a sigh of relief when Biggie yawned and picked up her bowl of peas. "I'm tired," she said. "I believe I'll just go in and have a little nap before supper."

Willie Mae got up and followed Biggie into the house. "I got to get my roast in the oven."

"I reckon I'll take a walk down to the feed store," Rosebud said, pitching his cigar butt into the yard. "I heard they got in some nice chrysanthemum flats this morning, and I aim to get some before they all picked over. Miss Biggie's got her heart set on bronze mums in that bed around her birdbath."

I got up from the steps and went to lie down on one of the big concrete buttresses that stand on either side of Biggie's front steps. The cement felt nice and warm from the sun. I was about to doze off when, plop, my cat, Booger, jumped down from the porch rail and landed right on top of me. I pressed his back with my hands until he settled down on my stomach, purring like a freight train. It was almost the end of summer. School would be starting in two more weeks. I was looking forward to the eighth grade. Life was good.

That was the last peaceful day we had that summer because the very next day an old friend of Biggie's showed up in town, and before we knew it, we were up to our necks in affairs we never should have been involved in. I blame Biggie for that. She just doesn't know how to keep her nose out of other folk's business.

1

Our next-door neighbor, Mrs. Moody, came tapping at the back door just as Willie Mae was frying up a batch of beignets for our breakfast. If you've never tasted beignets, you're in for a treat. They're little square doughnuts covered all over in powdered sugar. When Willie Mae puts them, hot out of the frying pan, on my plate then dusts them with enough powdered sugar to make them white as snow, I feel like I've died and gone to heaven.

"I just got a call from Woodrow," Mrs. Moody said, pouring herself a cup of coffee from the pot on the stove. She pulled out a chair and took a seat beside Biggie at the table. "Umm, something smells good. What is that, Willie Mae?"

"Beignets," Willie Mae said, not looking around.

"Have some breakfast with us," Biggie said. "What did Woodrow have on his mind this time?"

Woodrow is Mrs. Moody's son who lives in Wascom, over near the Louisiana line. To hear Mrs. Moody tell it, he would be president of General Motors if his wife wasn't holding him back. She says that's what you get when you marry beneath your station in life, a no-account wife and a house full of bucktoothed kids to support. Woodrow had to take a job delivering Rainbo bread to support his family instead of becoming a business tycoon the way he'd planned.

"It's Imogene, of course," Mrs. Moody said. "It seems her mother, who lives over in Marshall, lost her job at the pants factory. She's a widow, you know, since the old man drank himself to death."

"Poor thing." Biggie wiped powdered sugar off her chin. "What's she going to do?"

"Oh, she got another job right away," Mrs. Moody said. "She hired on with the gas company as a meter reader. That's the problem."

"How so?" Biggie asked.

"Well, it seems she was reading the gas meter outside the old folks home with a cigarette in her mouth. She didn't know the meter had a leak. Well, naturally the thing blew up—knocked the whole back wall out of the home, and several of the old folks went into heart failure from the shock. They said it shook cans off the shelves down at the Piggly Wiggly five blocks away."

"Was she killed?" I asked.

"Not her." Mrs. Moody held up her plate and waited while Willie Mae slid two fresh beignets on it. "That old woman is tough as boot leather. It singed off all her hair though, and she had burns on her face and arms. Anyway, now she's laid up in the hospital over in Marshall, and Imogene's got to go take care of her. Woodrow asked me to come look after him and the kids while she's away. Willie Mae, you've got to give me your recipe for these." She waved a beignet in the air over her head.

"Well, Essie, that's too bad. Is there anything I can do to help?" Biggie asked.

"Oh no, not a thing." Mrs. Moody got up and poured herself a fresh cup of coffee. "I was going to ask J.R. for one teensy favor though." She looked at me over her shoulder.

"What?" I asked.

"It's Prissy. I can't take her with me. Those children just run her ragged, all the time wanting to dress her up in doll clothes and push her around in that little toy stroller they've got. Prissy was a bundle of nerves the last time we visited them. I had to call up Doc Lasky over in Center Point to give her some pills to calm her down."

"Dr. Lasky's not a vet. He's a chiropractor—or an osteopath—something like that. Lonie Thedford said he did wonders for her last winter when she slipped and hurt her back."

"Oh, I know, Biggie. That man's got magic hands; everybody says so. But those pills he gave me sure did help Prissy. She calmed down real quick and slept for a day and a half, poor thing. She was just a wreck!"

To my way of thinking, Prissy is a nervous wreck all the time. She is a little white poodle, and all she ever does is run back and forth along her fence yapping at everybody who walks down the sidewalk. Even when she's asleep, she twitches and barks and makes running motions with her legs. My dog, Bingo, who is a mutt but ten times smarter than Prissy, is scared of her on account of she bit him once just because he was trying to get one little taste of the bone she was gnawing.

"I don't know," I said. "Booger and Bingo don't get along with her too good." The truth is, Booger can beat her up anytime he feels like it.

"Of course we'll take care of her," Biggie said. "J.R., you can keep her in that pen Rosebud built for Bingo when he was a puppy. When will you bring her over, Essie?"

"First thing tomorrow morning." Mrs. Moody stood up and brushed the powdered sugar off her blouse. "And I'll make it worth your while, J.R."

I remembered the last time she'd said that. I spent the whole afternoon raking up leaves in her yard, and she paid me with an old catcher's mitt that used to belong to Woodrow. It had a hole in the pocket with the stuffing coming out. I sighed, knowing there was no sense in arguing about it. Biggie's word is law in our house. I'd just have to find a way to keep Prissy in that pen and out of my hair most of the time. I nodded and went to the stove and held out my plate for another hot biegnet.

After breakfast, I rode my bike down to the vacant lot on the alley behind Handy's House of Hardware. It used to be a construction site on account of Mr. Handy was going to build a lumberyard there; but the bank wouldn't approve his loan, so now it's just this monster hole. Mr. Handy said us guys could build a dirt track out there as long as we didn't get hurt. When I got there, DeWayne Boggs, Arthur Handy, and Bruce Oterwald were dragging a huge piece of plywood from the back of the hardware store.

"Hey, J.R.," DeWayne said, dropping his end of the plywood, "looky here what we found."

"Cool," I said. "Does Mr. Handy know you've got that?"

"Yep," Arthur said.

"He gave it to us," Bruce put in. "See, it's warped in the middle, and the layers are coming apart at the corners on account of it got left out in the rain last week. We're gonna make a dirt bike ramp."

I pitched in and helped build the ramp. We laid it up against the side of the excavation, being careful to dig a trench and put rocks around the bottom edge so it wouldn't slide around. After it was set in place, we spent the rest of the morning racing our bikes up to the top. It felt great flying off the top of that old plywood, and it didn't hurt too much when we toppled down into the soft mud in the bottom of the hole. My bike and I were both pretty much of a mess when I rode into our yard around eleven.

As soon as I came in the back door, I noticed something was wrong. There was no smell of lunch being prepared, and Willie Mae was not even in the kitchen getting ready to cook anything. I went to the back stairs and yelled, "Biggeeee!"

Biggie appeared at the top of the stairs in her slip, her hand at her throat. "My soul, J.R., what's the matter?"

"Willie Mae's not cooking lunch," I said.

If looks could kill, I'd have been a dead duck. "J.R., you scared me half to death. Willie Mae had an emergency. Miss Rosa Dorsett, who goes to her church, has passed on, and Willie Mae had to go to the funeral home to fix her hair." Then she took a good look at me. "What on earth have you been doing? Get up here and get in the bathtub this very minute—and take off those shoes and leave them on the back porch. Willie Mae will have your hide if you leave a mess in her kitchen."

I left my clothes in a pile on the bathroom floor. I was just slipping into a clean tee shirt when Biggie tapped on the door, then without waiting for an answer, pushed it open and poked her head in. She had changed from her old sweat pants to a pantsuit with a scarf.

"How come you're so dressed up?" I asked before she could speak.

"That's just what I wanted to talk to you about." She leaned against the door frame. "I'm meeting some of the girls down at Mattie's Tea Room for lunch. You can come along if you want." Then she spotted my clothes on the floor and pointed. "Were you planning to leave those there?"

"Well, I didn't want to put them in the hamper with Willie Mae's clean dirty clothes."

"Probably a good idea," she said. "Take them out back and hang them on the clothesline. When we get back, you can wash the mud off with the hose."

"I might not go, Biggie."

"Suit yourself," she said, "but today's Tuesday, and Mattie's special is always fried catfish on Tuesday. Still, if you want to stay here, there's some leftover cornbread and turnip greens in the fridge. Just be sure to clean up after yourself."

"I guess I'll go." I picked up my muddy clothes and started down the backstairs. "I sure hope nobody sees me though."

Lately, I've been getting a little embarrassed about being seen all over town with my grandmother. I don't know why; I didn't used to feel that way. And that's not all. A lot of other things have been bothering me recently, like girls. All of a sudden, the girls in my class at school have taken to wearing lipstick and eye shadow and stuff. And the way they dress is real stupid, too. Half the time you can see their bare skin sticking out from between their pants and tops. And they're always whispering and looking at you out of the corners of their eyes. I don't know why that makes me nervous, but it does. Thank goodness my friend, Monica Sontag, doesn't act that way. If she ever starts, she can just kiss our friendship good-bye.

Mattie's Tea Room sits on the square right across Pecan Street from the courthouse. It is between Dossie's New and Old Antiques & Massage Parlor and Mr. Beamis's law office. Mrs. Mattie Thripp and her husband, Norman, run it, although if you ask me, I'd say Norman Thripp is nothing but a slave around there the way his wife orders him around all the time. If I ever get married, which I'm not going to, I'll never let my wife treat me the way Mattie treats Norman.

The tearoom is one of those girly places, if you know what I mean. Ruffled curtains hang on the windows, and the tables are covered with peach-colored cloths with little vases of fresh flowers in the middle of each one. Butch

Hinckley, who owns Hinckley's House of Flowers, changes the flowers every day or so. The chairs are all antiques, according to Miss Mattie, and I think she's telling the truth because most of them are pretty rickety.

A little silver bell tinkled when we pushed open the door and went inside. Mrs. Muckleroy, Miss Julia Lockhart, and Butch were already seated at the round table in the middle of the room. A long table under the windows had a white card in the middle that said RESERVED.

"Yoo-hoo, Biggie. Here we are," Miss Julia called out, as if we couldn't see them plain as day. "Oh, goody, J.R. came along. My stars, baby, you're getting tall just like your daddy." She turned to Butch. "Royce was our star basketball player when he was in high school. Remember, Ruby?"

Mrs. Muckleroy nodded, but didn't comment.

Butch was wearing a black tee shirt with a sequin chrysanthemum on the front and very tight white jeans with white tennies. "Ya'll sit down," he said, waving us toward the two empty chairs. "I've got to get back to the shop just as soon as I eat. I had to lock it up to come here since I don't have help anymore."

"I guess you're lost now that Meredith Michelle is on her glamorous honeymoon in the Bahamas." Mrs. Muckleroy held up her hand and examined her blood red fingernails.

Meredith Michelle is Mrs. Muckleroy's daughter and had worked for Butch before she got married last week. The wedding was the biggest party anybody's ever seen in Job's Crossing. At least that's what Mrs. Muckleroy says. She put up a big white tent in her backyard with a

15

floor for dancing. I heard her tell Biggie it was the only wedding ever in our town to have a live band. Some band. It was just Buddy Green, who is still in high school, and his garage band, which is named Snot Licks. The name is painted in big red letters on their bass drum. Mrs. Muckleroy made him cover that name with paper when he played for the wedding—and she introduced the band as Buddy and the Swing Kings. Buddy said he never would have sat still for that, but this was the first time they'd ever been asked to play anywhere. He thought the wedding might lead to future gigs.

Butch rolled his eyes at Mrs. Muckleroy's last remark. "Well, Ruby, if you want to know the truth . . ."

"What looks good?" Biggie asked quickly, picking up her menu. "Hmmm, Mattie's got crab quiche today. I might just have that, with a fresh green salad."

"We don't have that anymore." Miss Mattie had just walked up to the table and pulled up a chair. "Norman discovered he didn't have any crabmeat, so he substituted sardines. Uggh! I had to throw the things out. They smelled up the whole kitchen. I have some nice pasta primavera though."

"I'll have that then," Biggie said.

Mrs. Muckleroy had the same thing, while Miss Julia and Butch decided on a club sandwich. Naturally, I ordered the catfish special.

"You'll like that, J.R.," Miss Mattie said. "The catfish is crusted with ground pecans and Parmesan cheese. It's a recipe I saw on the Food Network."

"Can't I just have cornmeal on mine?" I asked.

"Are you sure, J.R.?" Miss Mattie asked. "It's very

good. We're serving it with a pureed red bell pepper sauce. Very elegant."

"Did *Emeril* do it?" Butch asked. "I just love that *Emeril. Bam!*" He picked up the salt shaker and pretended to sprinkle salt on the table.

"I'll just have the cornmeal," I said, "with ketchup."

Just as Miss Mattie started toward the kitchen to turn in our orders, the little bell over the door tinkled. "Oh, there's my party of ten," she said. "I'll just turn in your orders before I take care of them." She leaned down and whispered. "They're from an exclusive spa outside of town."

Biggie always taught me it was rude to stare, but you should have seen Biggie and Butch and Miss Julia and Mrs. Muckleroy staring at the new people. Their eyes like to have fallen right out of their heads. I've got to admit, I stared, too.

First came two youngish women, both thin as whispers. One had a sweet, round face with soft curls falling around it. She was wearing a sundress made of some kind of thin, floaty material. The other was the sporty type, if you know what I mean. She had short, brown hair and was very suntanned. She wore brown slacks with a cream-colored blouse and no makeup. Following them came eight teenage girls, and they sure weren't thin. Every one of them would've had a hard time sitting down in a number-three washtub. The girls were all wearing navy blue walking shorts and white blouses with red bandannas around their necks. They lumbered in and took seats at the long sides of the table. I worried about Miss Mattie's antique chairs. The two skinny ladies sat at the head and foot of the table. Before they sat down, one of the fat girls, the redheaded one, looked right at me and stuck out her tongue. I don't know why. I wasn't doing anything to her. Well, maybe I was staring just a little bit. I couldn't help it. I'd never seen anything like that in my whole life.

"Well, I'll be switched," Biggie said, when she could finally pry her eyes away.

"I'll bet I know who they are," Butch said. "I'll bet those are the folks from out at the Barnwell ranch. Only it's not called that anymore. Now it's called the Bar-LB. Get it? Bar-LB? Bar pounds? It's a fat farm. I think that's right clever, don't you, Biggie?"

"I guess." Biggie picked up her glass and took a quick sip of water. "Has, uh, has the place sold?"

"Biggie, you mean you didn't know?" Miss Julia shot Mrs. Muckleroy a glance. "Why, I would have personally come and told you myself if I'd had any idea."

"Well, Julia, why don't you just tell me now."

"Let me tell her." Mrs. Muckleroy looked like she'd just won the lottery. "Biggie, Rex Barnwell has moved back home!"

Biggie turned white as a sheet. Her hand shook as she reached for her water glass. "And, uh, and he's turned his daddy's ranch into a fat farm?"

"No, not him," Miss Julia said, "his wife."

"His *young* wife," Mrs. Muckleroy said. "I'll bet that's her sitting right over there—the pretty one, I mean."

Just then, Mr. Norman Thripp came over, bringing our food on a large tray. Miss Mattie trotted along behind him. "Norman, if you drop that, I'll kill you," she said, then turned to us. "I told him to make two trips, but *no,* Mr. *macho* man wants to take it all in one load."

Mr. Thripp set the tray down carefully on the table next to ours then started setting our food in front of us after asking who had what. When he finally had time to look around the room, he spotted the party of ten at the table by the window. He looked like he'd just peed on an electric fence. "Wha——What's, I mean, who're they?" he asked.

"Go on back to the kitchen, Norman, before they see you gaping. I'll explain later." Miss Mattie took her ticket book out of the pocket of her frilly apron and went to take their orders then came back and sat at our table.

"I'll be switched," she said. "Do you know every single one of them ordered just the garden salad? How do they expect a person to stay in business with orders like that?"

"Well, after all, they are on a diet." Biggie took a bite of her pasta. "Mattie, do you have any of that raspberry tea?"

"Sure. Anybody else?" They all said yes but me. I ordered a Big Red. Miss Mattie went to fetch the drinks.

"I know all about the place," Butch said. "I have to go out there every week and take fresh flowers for the main house."

"Tell us, Butch." Miss Julia writes for the local newspaper. "Maybe I should put something in my column."

"Well," Butch said, "first of all, the old man, Mr. Rex, is in real poor health. He hardly comes out of his room. Ya'll know, he used to be a famous race car driver—designed the Barnwell Baracuda back in the sixties. Natu-

19

rally, I don't know much about race cars, but they say it was real fast."

"We know all that, Butch." Mrs. Muckleroy put down her fork and glared at him. "Tell us about the young wife. Is she a bimbo?"

"Judge for yourself," Butch said. "That's her sitting right over there—the one in the dress."

"My soul," Biggie said, "she can't be over thirty. Rex is, let me see, Rex would be sixty-six by now."

"Where have you been, Biggie?" Miss Julia said. "They're doing it all the time—old codgers marrying young women. Look at Michael Douglas; look at Warren Beatty."

"Look at Alvis Turnipseed out at Rocky Mound," Butch said. "He married a girl thirteen."

"So what about the fat farm?" Biggie asked.

Butch looked at his rhinestone watch. "Okay, but I've got to tell it fast. They turned the bunkhouse into a dormitory and added on a gym and weight room, and they built a brand-new horse barn and dog kennels. It seems that Mrs. Barnwell and Grace Higgins—that's her, that other woman over there—have some new ideas for helping teenage girls with weight problems. They call it 'Earth-Spirit Renewal,' whatever that means! They do a lot of odd things like, for instance, they think it helps for the girls to care for animals."

"I don't see anything wrong with that," Biggie said.

"I didn't say there was anything wrong with it, did I?" Butch pushed his plate away then turned his chair sidewise, crossed his legs, and pointed his toes. "All I'm saying is, it's different. They spend a lot of time outside

20

at night, too. They call it 'moon bathing,' think they draw positive energy from the moon."

"Ooh, this is getting strange," Miss Julia said.

"That's not the strangest part," Butch said with a giggle. "They moon bathe in the raw. Oscar D. Hayes, who has the farm next door, saw them one night when he was out looking for a fox that had been getting at his chickens. They were all lined up on blankets on the side of a hill. Oscar said his dog, Prince, ran under the house and wouldn't come out until four o'clock the next afternoon after seeing that. Oscar said he was pretty shaken up about it his own self."

"So what's wrong with Rex?" Biggie asked.

"Lots of things," Butch said. "One thing is, he had his leg amputated on account of his diabetes, but I think his heart's bad, too."

"Come, J.R." Biggie got up suddenly. "I think I've heard enough."

I had to run to keep up with Biggie, she got out of there so fast.

2

Rosebud is my substitute daddy. He is also my best friend in the whole wide world. He has taught me all I know about fishing and hunting, and he even coaches my baseball team. And he never ever gets mad at me even when I do something really dumb. That's why I was so surprised when he near about bit my head off today. Here is how it happened.

Biggie went right up to her room and closed the door as soon as we got back from the tearoom. She wouldn't come out even though I banged on her door and called her name a bunch of times. Finally, after about the tenth time, she hollered at me to go away and leave her alone. Well, I don't have to tell you that really hurt my feelings. I went looking for Willie Mae, but she hadn't come back from the funeral home yet, so I just went into my room to play video games while Booger sat on the floor trying to bat the moving figures with his paw. After about an hour of that, I got hungry and so did Booger, so we went downstairs to see what we could find to eat. Rosebud was in the kitchen stirring a pot of red beans on the stove.

"How come Willie Mae's not cooking?"

"She went over to Mrs. Rosa Dorsett's house to stay with her family for a spell. It seems they all pretty upset about losing they mama and all."

"So what are we supposed to do? Starve?"

Rosebud turned around and gave me a look. "What do it look like *I'm* doing?"

"Cooking beans. What else are we having?"

"Cornbread and buttermilk."

"Rosebud, that's not a meal!"

"It's a fine meal for plenty of folks, young'un, and you'd best be proud you got it."

That hurt my feelings, but that's not the worst part. The worst part came after we'd eaten our cornbread and beans and went out to the front porch to sit while Rosebud smoked his cigar. Biggie never came down for supper.

Figuring to lighten the mood, I decided to tell Rosebud a funny story. "Rosebud, you should have seen what I saw today."

"What?" He put his feet up on the porch rail and blew a fat smoke ring.

"I saw eight fat girls down at the tearoom. Ooo-wee, they were so funny. They jiggled every time they moved, and when they got up to leave, their butts looked like two hogs fighting in a tow sack." I got the giggles just thinking about it and about rolled off my chair laughing.

When I finally caught my breath, I looked at Rosebud to see if he was laughing, too.

He wasn't. He was glaring at me.

"Boy," he said in a tone I'd never heard, "I never thought I'd be ashamed of you, but right this minute, I can't hardly look at you."

"Me? Why? It was funny, Rosebud. One of um liked to have broke one of Miss Mattie's antique chairs, and her old butt just hung over the edge. Rosebud, why are you looking at me that way?"

"I oughta burn your butt, that's why. Ain't I taught you nothin'?"

I was getting scared, the way he was looking at me. "I'm sorry, Rosebud. What did I do?"

"You made fun of somebody that can't help the way they is."

Now I was getting mad. "They can help it! They don't have to eat so much."

"Ain't none of your business how much they eats."

We sat there for a long time not talking. I was trying to figure out what I'd done to upset Rosebud so. Finally, he spoke.

"I ever tell you about my uncle Eroy Robichaux?"

"Uh-uh."

"Uncle Eroy was the sweetest feller you could ever hope to meet—and the fattest. He spend most of his days settin' on an old sofa on my grandmomma's front porch. He had arms the size of hams, and his face had swelled up to the size of a pumpkin. He didn't have no neck a'tall. He stayed on that couch all day long. Only time he'd get up was when he had to make his way down to the out-house, which was about fifty yards from the house. Even then, he'd have to hold on to a fence post to rest on the way there and back. He'd get so out of breath, doncha know.

"But he was a kind man. Everybody loved Uncle Eroy—even the animals. Them old dogs would just lay around his feet all day. Even the chickens would come up and set on his knees. Once, I saw a mockingbird fly down and take a chunk of bread right out of his hand."

"Did he sleep out there, too?"

"Course not. At night, he slept on a mattress on the floor what my grandmomma had fixed up for him after his bed broke down."

"Why didn't he go on a diet?"

"Oh, Uncle Eroy didn't eat that much. Oh, he might have four or five eggs for breakfast with several biscuits and a couple of slices of ham, but he wasn't what you might call a real heavy eater. We all ate like that on account of we worked so hard. No, it was something else that made Uncle so fat. Glands, or something, I expect."

"Glands can make you fat?"

"Oh, sure. And sometimes, it's in your genes. You know, like all your family's got the same problem."

"I never knew that."

"I know. You just wants to make fun of people, don't you?"

"I said I was sorry, Rosebud."

"Okay. So, anyway, every week or so, Miss Marie Guidry from up the road would drop by to pass the time of day with Eroy. Sometimes she'd bring along a cake or some cookies she'd baked. Uncle Eroy loved her something awful."

"I bet she didn't love him back though—him being so fat and all."

"Miss Marie was kind and gentle. She loved everybody, so I guess she loved Uncle Eroy, too. But if you mean in a marryin' way, well no, she didn't. Miss Marie was the most popular gal in the parish. She could of married anybody she wanted to."

"Poor Uncle Eroy."

Rosebud ignored that remark. "One spring day, Uncle Eroy was settin' on his couch enjoying the morning sun when he got the urge to visit the outhouse. Wellsir, he picked up his walking stick and hoisted himself up off of the couch and, holding on to the porch pillars, he edged himself down to the ground then slowly, slowly made his way down the path to the privy."

"Is this going to get interesting?"

"Hush, boy, and lemme tell this. After Uncle Eroy got through with his business and was standing out in the sun again, he taken a notion to take himself a little walk. Just a few steps, doncha know, to see if he could. So instead of going back to the house like he always did, he turned toward the woods that run along behind the privy and looked down the little cow path that led right into them woods."

Just then a car stopped in front of the house and Willie Mae got out. She came up to the front of the house but didn't come up to the porch.

26

"Hey, honey," Rosebud said. "How's Mr. Dorsett and them?"

"Taking it hard." Willie Mae wiped her brow with the back of her hand. "Law me, I'm tired. I must have cooked for thirty people or more. The whole family and then some were over at that house." She looked at me. "You get any supper?"

I had just opened my mouth to speak when Rosebud kicked me hard on the ankle. "I, uh—oh, yeah. Rosebud made us some beans and cornbread. It was good!"

"Fine then. I'm plumb wore out. I'll see you in the morning." With that, she turned and walked around the side of the house to her little cottage out back. After we heard the screen door slam shut, Rosebud continued.

" 'I'll just take mebbe two, three steps,' Uncle Eroy thought. So slowly, slowly, holding on to the privy door, he put one foot out, then another and another, grunting with every step on account of it was such a effort, moving them old heavy legs of his. He got to concentratin' so hard on moving one foot in front of the other that he forgot to look and see how far he'd gone. When he did stop and hold on to a sweet gum tree to catch his breath, he was surprised to see that he'd come a good twenty yards from the outhouse. He was near about to the edge of the woods."

"So then did he start back?"

"No. It was a funny thing. Uncle Eroy felt a sense of power come over him. 'I done gone this far,' he thought, 'lemme see can I go just a little bit farther.' Well, to make a long story short, he kept on walking 'til he found himself deep in the woods and tired. That man was plumb wore out. He was scared to sit down on the ground on account of he might not be able to get back up."

"He probably couldn't," I said.

"You right," Rosebud said. "Well, before long, he found a dead tree laying across the path, so he just taken a seat on that to rest. Away off, he could hear Grand-momma and them calling for him. Uncle Eroy said he never did understand why he didn't answer them. Something just told him to keep on walking, so after he rested awhile, he got up and commenced putting one foot after the other again."

"How far did he go, Rosebud?"

"Oh, he went quite a good little ways. Uncle Eroy walked from St. Martinville to New Iberia and then on down to Jeanerette."

"Golly!"

"Oh, that ain't all. He crossed the bayou at Morgan City and kept on walking."

"How did he eat? Where did he sleep?"

"Ate whatever he could find along the way: berries, crawfish, caught him a fish now and then."

"I'll bet he lost some of that weight. Right, Rosebud?"

"You betcha. By the time he got to New Orleans, Uncle Eroy was plumb rawboney. He was tall, too. Did I tell you that?"

I shook my head.

"Oh, yeah, cher, Uncle Eroy would have gone six feet or more."

"So what did he do next? Go back home?"

"Nope. He went and got him a job working the docks.

He found him a little room to rent and stayed there near 'bout half a year. Made hisself some good money, too. Still and all, Uncle Eroy wasn't too crazy about city life what with the noise and lights, and he said he was gettin' right tired of them smelly old docks, so he took a notion to move on. First, he bought himself a good pair of walkin' boots though."

"Back home?"

"Well, not at first. Uncle Eroy figured he had missed a lot spending his days settin' on that couch. He wanted to see a little more of the world. What he done was, he left New Orleans goin' east. What he didn't know was, he was about to get a surprise."

"What surprise?"

"It happened just after he'd passed through Slidell." Rosebud took a fresh cigar out of his pocket. "Run get me a cup of coffee, will you?"

I hurried inside to the kitchen and took Rosebud's favorite coffee mug with a picture of the *Dixie Queen* on it and poured thick black coffee out of the pot on the stove. It smelled awful. When I got back with the coffee, Rosebud was puffing on his cigar. "What surprise?"

"He seen a sign, that's what."

"You mean an omen, like Willie Mae sees?"

"Naw. It was a sign. It said WELCOME TO MISSISSIPPI."

"Oh."

"Well, you see, Uncle Eroy didn't want to go to Mississippi. He figured he ain't seen all of his own home state yet. So he turned around and headed back home, only this time he turned north so he could pass through Baton Rouge, thinking he might like to take a look at the state

29

capital. Then, after he'd seen enough, he cut through the swamp to Beaux Bridge and from there it wasn't but a little way home. By the time the first frost came, he'd done made it back."

"What's that got to do with anything?"

"Everything. You see, his folks was so glad to see him, they killed a hog and roasted it over an open fire. The party went on for four whole days with singin' and dancin' and quite a little bit of drinkin' and eatin'."

"What finally happened to Uncle Eroy?"

"Oh, he married Miss Marie Guidry and they had seven kids, all girls, before Uncle Eroy fell out of a pirogue, hit his head on a rock, and drowned himself in the bayou."

We sat for a long time not talking while Rosebud sipped his coffee and smoked his cigar. Finally, I had to ask a question. "Rosebud, was that story supposed to tell me something? Because I don't see what it has to do with those fat girls at the tearoom."

"You don't?"

"Uh-uh."

"Well, what did Uncle Eroy do first?"

"He decided to take a walk?"

"Boy, are you thick or something? He had to take that first step is what. That first step took the most courage. Seems to me that's what those girls did when they went to that there diet place. Now Uncle Eroy, he kept right on puttin' one foot in front of the other until he got where he wanted to be. That took determination. Only time will tell whether them girls got what it takes to make it, but you ain't got no call to be jokin' around about them because you ain't got any idea what you'd do in their place."

"I guess you're right, Rosebud. But I wish Uncle Eroy hadn't died."

"Him? He was gonna die soon anyway. He was eighty-seven when he drowned in the bayou. Now, get on up to bed. It's past your bedtime."

I pounded on Biggie's door when I got upstairs, but she wouldn't answer.

"Biggie," I called "Biggie, are you okay."

When she answered, I could have sworn she was crying. "Go away, J.R. I'll see you in the morning."

3

The next morning when I came down for breakfast, Biggie was sitting at the table drinking coffee. She was still wearing her nightgown and robe. I hadn't seen her do that since she had the flu last winter. Biggie always says she can't think straight unless she is dressed properly for the day. When she looked up at me, her eyes had as many red lines as a Mississippi road map. She managed to give me a half smile then shoved her cup toward Willie Mae for a refill.

I sat down beside Biggie. "You okay, Biggie?"

She rumpled my hair. "Sure, honey. Just a tiny little headache, that's all." She shook herself and sat up straighter. "Why don't we have chicken spaghetti for supper tonight, Willie Mae? It's been quite a while since we had that."

Willie Mae cracked an egg into a saucer and slid it

into a pan of simmering water. "You want spinach salad or coleslaw with that?" She slid another egg into the water.

Biggie drummed her fingers on the table. "You know what I'd really like? I'd like some of that wilted lettuce you make. You know, the kind with hard-boiled eggs and bacon?"

Willie Mae took the eggs out of the pan with a slotted spoon and laid them on my plate, blotting them off with paper towels. Next she added a slice of country-cured ham and two fat fluffy biscuits fresh from the oven. She set the plate in front of me.

"Yuk," I said, looking down at my plate.

"How come you say that?" Rosebud asked. He was spooning down his poached eggs like they were good and sopping up the juice with a biscuit.

"I was hoping for some gingerbread pancakes."

"Put some butter on them eggs and they go down better." Rosebud shoved the butter dish toward me. "Uh-oh, there goes the phone."

Biggie got up from the table and answered the phone at her little kitchen desk. "Hello? Oh hey, Coye. . . . Um-hmm. . . . Say what? . . . Well, sure. We'd love to have her. . . . Fine. . . . Okay. We'll see you around two then."

"Was that Mr. Sontag?" I asked.

"Yep. He has to take Ernestine over to Longview to the eye doctor this afternoon. They won't be back until late, so they wanted to know if Monica could spend the night with us."

"Yeah!" I said. Monica and her family live on the farm Biggie grew up on. Monica is my best friend next to Rosebud even though she does only have hair on one side of her head on account of being left too close to the fire when she was a baby. Monica is the only girl in the world I can talk to and that's only because she's so much like a boy. She's not afraid of the devil himself. I know that for a fact.

About that time the back door swung open and in walked Mrs. Moody. She was dressed in a bright blue pantsuit with a black crocheted hat on her head. She carried Prissy under one arm. In her other hand she had a cloth shopping bag, which she set down on Biggie's desk next to the back stairs. She set Prissy on the floor by her feet and began pulling things out of the bag. Prissy leaned against her ankles, trembling.

Mrs. Moody dug down into the bag and pulled out a pottery bowl with PRISSY written in blue on its side. "This is her water bowl," she said. "The little darling knows it, too. Just don't bother trying to put her food in this bowl. She won't touch a bite of it." She looked at me to make sure I understood. I nodded. "And this is her Snookums." She took out a faded old rag doll. "She sleeps with her head on Snookums every single night. Oh, and here's her food bowl." It was identical to the water bowl with her name on the side and everything.

"How am I supposed to know the difference?" I asked.

Mrs. Moody knit her brows like she was thinking hard. "Well, I hadn't thought of that. They are just exactly alike. I got them over at Marshall Pottery. Here's an idea. Why don't you put her water in one bowl, and if she won't drink it, you'll know that's her food bowl. Well,

34

I've got to scoot. I told Ace Redfearn to be at my front door with his taxi at eight-thirty. Oh, yes, and I've left her bed with her fuzzy blanket on the back porch." She came over and pinched my cheek. "I know I can count on you to take good care of my baby."

"Yes'm. I guess."

Mrs. Moody picked up Prissy and set her in my lap. "Now you be a good girl, hear?"

Prissy growled and I saw that Booger had come into the kitchen and was sitting by the stove licking himself. *This is going to be interesting,* I thought, *and might turn out to be fun.* As soon as I made sure Mrs. Moody was gone, I pushed Prissy off my lap. She immediately started in yapping at Booger, who looked at her like she was a gnat and went right on licking his bottom. After a while, I guess Booger got tired of it because, quick as a flash, he reached out his paw and boxed Prissy on the nose, then walked off down the hall with his tail high. Prissy crawled under the desk, lay down, and tucked her nose between her two front paws.

"J.R., go outside and make sure that pen you built for Bingo is still secure. If it isn't, fix it; if it is, put Prissy out there. Make sure you give her plenty of water and put her bed and a blanket in the little doghouse." Biggie held on to the table when she stood up. "I think I'll just go up and rest a little longer. I didn't sleep too well last night." She looked at me again. "You might want to put Snookums out there, too. Poor little thing; she's going to be lonely for Essie."

"Yes'm."

It took me a whole hour to get Prissy situated because

the hog wire we'd built the pen out of had stretched in places. I got some wire out of the garage and mended the holes and filled what I hoped was her water bowl. I threw in a couple of Bingo's milk bones along with her stupid rag doll.

When I got back inside, Prissy wasn't under the desk where I'd left her. Rosebud was still at the table enjoying a second cup of coffee, and Willie Mae had joined him.

"Did y'all see where Prissy went?" I asked.

"Nope." Rosebud set down his coffee cup and began cleaning his fingernails with his pocketknife.

"Don't be doing that at the table," Willie Mae said. "That's nasty."

Rosebud grinned and put away his knife.

"Willie Mae, did you see which way she went?"

"When do I got time to go keeping tabs on a dog?"

I searched the house for Prissy. I looked under the couch in the parlor then behind the piano. I looked behind all the doors and under all the beds. She wasn't anywhere. I even looked in all the closets and up in the attic. Prissy was nowhere to be found. Finally, I went out in the yard and yelled my lungs out for her. I even checked the neighbors' yards on both sides of the street. No Prissy. Now I was getting pretty worried. Even though she was, to my way of thinking, a poor excuse for a dog, I didn't want anything bad to happen to her.

It was after eleven when I finally gave up and came back in the house. Biggie, dressed and looking much better, was talking on the telephone in the hall.

"They want us to come today? That's pretty short notice, isn't it?" She listened for a long time. "Umm . . . you forgot. . . . Is Butch going? . . . He is. . . . How about Ruby? . . . Oh, well, I guess. I'll meet you at the square at three then. Okay. Bye." She hung up the phone and saw me standing there for the first time. "Oh, J.R., some of us are invited out to the Barnwell ranch for tea this afternoon. I want you to go along."

"Me? Why? I don't want to go, Biggie. There's nothing but a bunch of fat girls out there. No guys or nothin'."

"J.R., I want you to go."

"No, ma'am, I'm not going. I got better things to do than tag along after you all the time." I was scared and shaking all over. I had never disobeyed Biggie before, but now was the time to take a stand. Biggie needed to realize that I was a teenager and not just a little kid anymore.

"It's important to me, J.R." There was a tremor in her voice.

I almost gave in. It wasn't going to hurt me to go with Biggie. I'd done it all my life and had some pretty interesting adventures doing it. I opened my mouth to say okay when something stopped me, something strong that seemed to be pulling me away from being a kid and into—something else. "NO!" I ran up to my room and slammed the door. I flung myself on my bed and lay there shaking all over. It seemed the walls might come tumbling down on top of me—my whole life might be breaking apart. What was wrong with Biggie? Why had she acted so funny last night? Did it have to do with all those fat girls at the tearoom? How could it? And what was wrong with me? I had never behaved like that in all my days with Biggie and Willie Mae and Rosebud— never ever wanted to.

I was still trying to figure it all out when I heard a tap on my door, then the door opened and Biggie peeked in. "May I come in?"

I was surprised. Biggie never asked that. She usually just walked right in.

I sat up on the bed and nodded. "Am I in trouble?"

"No." Biggie sat on the edge of the bed and patted my leg. "I have a story to tell you. I never thought you'd have to know, but now I guess you do."

I sat up against the headboard pushing a pillow behind my back. "Yes'm."

4

"Job's Crossing was a whole different place when I was a girl than it is today." Biggie crossed her legs Indian style and sat facing me on the bed.

"How's that?"

"For one thing, there were four cafés downtown and a shoeshine parlor and a newsstand."

"No foolin'?"

"No foolin'. And every Saturday night, the stores stayed open until ten o'clock so that all the farmers could come into town to do their business."

"Way cool." If anybody had asked me, I would have said the town was quieter in the olden days, not livelier.

"Not only that, we had two picture shows on the square—two! One was old and dirty and showed mostly cowboy movies and serials, while the other, which was just a little nicer, showed the first-run movies. Every Sunday afternoon, my friends and I would wear our church dresses to the matinee."

"You dressed up to go to the movies?"

"Well, yes, but only on Sundays. That's the way everybody did things back then. And the ladies all wore hats and gloves even if they were just going to the grocery store. Everything was more formal in those days."

"That's lame."

"It's just the way things were. People set a greater store on their reputation in the community and who their family was than how kind they were or how honorable." Biggie looked out the window for a long time until I began to get uncomfortable. I wondered why she was telling me all this.

"What kind of movies did they show?"

"Oh, you know. You've seen old movies on television. When I was a child the war was on, and we mostly saw movies about that. People were very patriotic."

"I've heard that word, but I'm not real sure I know what it means."

"It means they talked a lot about how great our country was—and how bad our enemies were. We had to, you know, support our soldiers in the war. We grew Victory Gardens in our backyards and saved tinfoil and cooking fat for the war effort. And the ladies all knitted socks and gloves for the soldiers. My daddy served on the draft board."

"Well the town sounds neat. I wish it was still that way—except for the dressing up part. The war sounds cool."

"The war wasn't cool at all. People were killed, J.R. And there were other bad things as well."

"Like what?"

"Well, for starters, the colored people all had to sit in the balcony when they went to the picture show—and they couldn't go in any of the cafés on the square."

"Why?"

"That's just the way things were in those days. And something else, you know that water fountain on the courthouse lawn?"

I nodded. "It doesn't work anymore."

"I know, but that's not the point. The point is there used to be two there, and they were marked with signs that said COLORED and WHITES. They tore the colored fountain down sometime in the seventies."

"Yeah, I know all about segregation. We studied civil rights and Martin Luther King Jr. in school. I know one thing, I'd a darn sight rather drink after Willie Mae than Cooter McNutt." Cooter McNutt lives in a cabin out on the banks of the creek. When he's in town, you can smell him coming a block away.

"I doubt if you know all about it. You had to be there. Someday, I'll tell you more. But that's not what we're here to talk about right now. Today we're going to talk about me. Did you know my father was once mayor of Job's Crossing?"

"No, ma'am. I thought your daddy was a farmer like Mr. Sontag. Didn't you grow up out on the farm?"

"Where did you get that idea, honey?" Biggie patted my knee.

41

"Because you're all the time talking about what fun you had out in the country."

"J.R., it was my *grandparents* who lived on the farm. I did spend a lot of time out there, but I grew up in this very house." She looked at the crepe myrtle tree covered with pink blooms outside my window. "In fact, this was my room. I used to look out at Ruby Muckleroy's house from this very window. She was Ruby Morris then, and we grew up together. Now you can't see the house anymore because this tree has grown so much. I remember when my daddy planted it here. It wasn't more than six feet tall. . . ."

She continued to look out the window not saying anything. Finally, I cleared my throat, and she looked at me like she'd just come back from somewhere far away.

"When I entered high school the war had been over for a number of years, but the veterans, those who made it through, were still coming home. Some had signed up for extra hitches in the service; some were injured and had to stay in service until their wounds healed. A few, those who quit school to join up, tried to go back to high school, but that never worked very well. How can you go by high school rules when you've seen people die on the battlefield?"

I shrugged my shoulders, wondering what this had to do with her wanting me to go out to that ranch with her.

"By the time I was a sophomore, most of the veterans had drifted away to go to college on the G.I. Bill or to take jobs at the steel mill. One stayed though." She smiled. "A good-looking fellow with coal black hair and light blue eyes. He had one little curl that kept falling down over his forehead no matter how much he combed it back with the little black comb he kept in his shirt pocket." She looked out the window some more then shook herself and spoke again. "He seemed so glamorous to all us girls. Most everybody had a crush on him at one time or another, even though our mothers had told us to steer clear of him. They didn't need to worry. He didn't pay any attention to us at all. I guess we seemed like babies to him. Some said he was dating a girl from Center Point."

"Biggie, Monica's going to be here pretty soon." I was hoping to speed this story up. Biggie ignored that remark.

"I had always been something of a tomboy, so I never paid as much attention to him as the other girls did. I was too interested in fishing and hunting and, most especially, horseback riding with my grandpa out on the farm. Then, between my sophomore and junior year, a funny thing happened."

"What, Biggie?" I was hoping this story was going to get interesting again.

"My skinny little body that had always been mostly elbows and knees changed. I began to get curves. Mama said I was a late bloomer, and I guess I was. Suddenly, I started thinking there might be more to life than horses. I began to pay more attention to my clothes and my hair. I went to the dime store and bought a powder compact, some Maybelline mascara, and a tube of bright orange Tangee lipstick." She smiled, thinking about herself at that age. "I wanted people to notice how I looked; but when they did notice, I squirmed and blushed."

Now I was really getting bored. I snuck a look at the clock beside the bed. Only fifteen minutes had passed since Biggie started this story. She saw me, of course.

"I know, honey. All this must seem pretty dull to you, but *you have to know.* I never thought you would, but now . . . well, circumstances have changed." She shifted to a more comfortable position on the bed. "That's when the boys started treating me differently. Where before we had played ball together and ridden our bikes out to the creek and climbed trees, now they wanted to ask me out on dates. And I liked it—a lot. I learned to dance the latest dances and to toss my head and flirt."

I tried to imagine Biggie flirting, but it was impossible.

"One night our crowd had gone as a group to the state park. The moon shone down on the dance pavilion. We were having a great time until someone played 'Stardust' on the jukebox."

"Huh?"

"It's a song, J.R. I was sitting outside watching the moon's reflection in the lake when I heard this voice asking me to dance. I turned around and it was *him,* the veteran. I hadn't even known he was there that night." She closed her eyes and continued to speak. "We danced that number, then another and another. I fit just right in his arms, and even though I wasn't such a good dancer, I could follow him perfectly."

I wanted to get up and run out of there. Why was Biggie telling me this?

"Finally my friends got ready to leave," she continued. "He asked me to stay with him, said he'd take me home when I was ready. I stayed even though I knew Papa would be furious if he found out. Papa needn't have worried. That boy was a perfect gentleman, taking my arm when we left the dance floor (the other boys just walked away and left you standing there), offering to buy me a Coke, pulling a chair out for me to sit down in. That night I fell in love, honey."

"Biggie, do I need to know all this?" I was getting more embarrassed by the minute.

She reached forward and squeezed my ankle. "J.R., you do. Now, you need to be patient. I'll try to make it shorter." She took a deep breath. "After that, we saw each other every chance we got. Of course, I had to sneak around. My daddy would have had a conniption fit. By the time this all happened, the young man had left high school and taken a temporary job at Mr. Brown's garage. He had plans to take a test to finish high school then go on to college and study mechanical engineering. He loved cars, but he didn't want to be a mechanic for the rest of his life." She smiled. "I saw him all that spring. We would slip off and go to the movies at Center Point or Gilmer. Sometimes he would take me over to Gladewater to the honky-tonks where we would dance. I felt so grown-up. He would have maybe one beer, but he never let me drink."

"And nobody found out?"

"The other kids knew, of course. The girls all thought it was great and used to cover for me, but the boys were different. They teased me a lot, and once I found a nasty slur written on my locker at school."

"Why?"

"Because they were jealous, I guess. I don't know. Maybe they thought I was, you know, having *relations* with him. I wasn't, though. That came later."

"Biggie!"

"My stars, J.R., you hear worse than this on TV every day!"

"I know, Biggie, but you're my grandmother. Give me a break!"

"Just be quiet and listen. In June, he got a letter saying he had been accepted to Texas A&M in the engineering department. I was glad for him but heartbroken that he would be leaving town. How I was going to miss him! I even thought of running away and finding a job in College Station just to be near him."

"Biggie! That was crazy!"

"I know. It was foolish, but someday, honey, you'll know how it feels to be in love for the very first time."

"Not me. I don't even think about girls."

She gave me a look then continued. "One night after we'd been to a movie, he asked me to marry him—later, he said, after he finished college. Well, when you're sixteen, four years is a lifetime. I burst into tears and said I couldn't wait that long. I was young and in love, and I wanted to be with him right then. We talked for hours that night. He tried to convince me that we could wait, that he could come back for visits, maybe even bring my parents around. I wasn't having any of that. I told him it was now or never, that I wouldn't wait for him."

"I guess you haven't changed very much, huh, Biggie?"

She smiled. "Well, I've always been hardheaded.

Anyway, finally he agreed. But he said he wouldn't take me with him unless we got married."

"Biggie, even I know you can't get married when you're sixteen."

"At that time you could in Arkansas. One day, we slipped off to Texarkana and got a marriage license. The next week, we were married by a justice of the peace. We went to Paris for our honeymoon—Paris, Texas!"

"And your parents didn't know?" I sneaked another peek at the clock. It was almost two.

"No. I had told them I was spending the night with a friend."

"So what did they say when you got back?"

"They never found out. After the honeymoon, I went back home and slept in my room just like before."

I looked around at my room with its solid green walls and sports posters and imagined what it must have been like when Biggie was a girl. In my mind, I saw flowered wallpaper—maybe ruffled curtains and a lace bedspread. I sighed and wondered if this room would ever feel the same to me again.

"Finally," she continued, "it was time for him to leave, and I was determined to go along. I packed my bags one night and slipped out of the house while Mama and Daddy slept."

"So what happened? Did you move to College Station?"

"Yes—for four days. That's how long it took my daddy to find me and bring me back. He threatened the boy with jail if he ever tried to see me again, and he could have made it stick because I was a minor."

"And that was it? You just came back home?"

"Almost. Daddy made me get divorced from him. I cried myself to sleep every night—wouldn't come out of my room for weeks. And I couldn't hold down food anymore. I lost so much weight, my parents threatened to put me in the hospital and have me fed by a tube. My parents arranged a marriage for me to Albert Wooten. He was the son of friends of theirs. I had always liked Albert, just not in *that* way, doncha know."

"Why, Biggie? Why'd they have to go and do that?"

"There was reason enough."

"And Albert? He agreed—just like that?"

"Albert wasn't a very forceful person, if you know what I mean. And he had always liked me a lot. I felt trapped, so I just gave in. I was just a kid, and I didn't see how I had any choice. But I promised myself then and there that nobody would ever force me to do anything against my will again—and they never have. We had a big church wedding and seven months later your daddy was born."

"Biggie! You mean . . ."

"That's right, honey. Your daddy was the child of the man I loved, the veteran, not Albert. Albert knew, of course, but he never threw it up to me. He was a quiet man, a good provider. He never interfered with anything I wanted to do—and he raised your daddy like his own. In the end I came to love him, but in a different way, if you know what I mean."

"When did Albert die?"

She looked at me. "Die? Albert didn't die as far as I know. One day, after your daddy grew up, he just got into his car and drove out of town. He left a piece of paper giving everything he owned to me—except one thousand dollars and the car he drove off in." She smiled. "I never even missed him. Isn't that funny? He used to send me postcards from places like Omaha and Boston, and he'd send money when he could. But after a time, the cards and letters stopped, and I never heard from him again."

I shook my head. "I always thought my granddaddy died. Whatever happened to the first guy?"

"Oh, I never saw him either, and finally the hurt healed. Once in a while, word would trickle back to town about something he had done. You see he became quite famous. He turned his love of cars into a career, first as a race car driver then later as a designer of new car prototypes."

I sat for a long time thinking about what Biggie had told me. "Wait a minute, Biggie. That guy, the man at the fat farm, they said he was a driver. Was he the veteran?"

"Yes, honey, Rex Barnwell is the veteran. That's why I had to tell you this story. Others know, and before long somebody would have told you. I wanted it to come from me."

"Biggie! That means Rex Barnwell is my granddaddy. Right?"

"Right. But he doesn't know it. Now may be the time for him to find out." She leaned over and gave me a hug. "Okay?"

I didn't answer.

"Okay?"

"I guess. What difference does it make anyway? He

doesn't know me, and I don't know him. But, Biggie, why are you so set on me going out there if he doesn't even know you had his baby?"

"I'm not sure myself," she said. "Something just tells me you two need to meet. Oops, there goes the doorbell. That must be Monica."

I slid off the bed and headed for the door. I had my hand on the doorknob when Biggie called my name.

"Yes'm?"

"We don't have to ever talk about this again if you don't want to."

I nodded. That was fine with me. I'd never wanted to talk about it in the first place.

5

What's wrong with you? You look like you just swallowed a frog." Monica was dressed in camouflage pants and a tee shirt. She had her baseball cap on backward.

"Worse than that," I said, "but I can't tell you. It's a Family Secret."

"Suit yourself," she said, heading for the kitchen. "What's Willie Mae making? It smells good!"

I followed her out to the kitchen where we found Willie Mae dropping spoonfuls of oatmeal cookie dough packed with raisins and pecans on a cookie sheet. Our noses told us a batch was already baking in the oven.

"Ooo-wee, Willie Mae, you're the best cook in the whole wide world," Monica said, sidling up to Willie Mae. "Can I have some raw dough?"

"It'll give you worms," Willie Mae said, hiding a smile. She likes Monica. "Set yourselves down at the table and hold your horses. I'll have you some ready directly."

We were just getting ready to plow into hot cookies and cold sweet milk when Biggie came down the backstairs. She was dressed in her new black pantsuit with a yellow, black, and white scarf. She even had on a pair of black, open-toed shoes.

"Hey, Miss Biggie, you look good enough to eat," Monica said around a mouthful of cookie.

"We're all invited to tea out at the Barnwell ranch," Biggie said. "Willie Mae, do you know where Rosebud went?"

"Last time I looked, he was washing the car." Willie Mae slid another pan of cookies into the oven. "What you want with him?"

"I want him to drive," she said. "We're taking Julia and Ruby along with us."

"Biggie," I said, "Prissy is lost."

"Lost? How?" Biggie bit into a chewy cookie.

"She's just disappeared. I've looked all over for her. Mrs. Moody's gonna kill me."

"She sure is." Monica drained her milk glass. "I've seen how she takes on over that dumb dog."

"You're pretty goofy over your dog," I said.

"Buster? Well, sure. He's an outstanding dog. Remember when he rescued us from the bottomless pit on Frontier Day that time? If it wasn't for Buster barking so much, we'd still be down there."

"I guess," I said. The way I remembered it, Buster had been the cause of our falling into the pit in the first place. But it's no good arguing with Monica.

"Never mind that now," Biggie said. "Go outside and tell Rosebud I'm ready to go."

"Where ya'll going, Miss Biggie?" Monica took another cookie off the plate.

"We're all going out to a ranch in the country," Biggie said. "We've been invited to tea."

Clouds were building up in the west when I went out to tell Rosebud. "It's gonna rain," I said.

" 'Course it is. I'm washing the car, ain't I?"

"Biggie's ready to go. Have you seen Prissy?"

"Ain't seen her. I reckon she'll show herself once it commences to rain. Tell Miss Biggie I'll be ready in fifteen minutes." He grabbed a towel and started wiping down Biggie's big black funeral limousine that she bought cheap off the undertaker over in Center Point after he bought a brand-new white one. Biggie bought it because she said now we could carry our fishing poles inside and not have to ride around with those poles sticking out the window and have everybody and his dog know where we were going.

After we picked up Mrs. Muckleroy and Miss Julia, Rosebud drove the car to the bypass then turned east onto Center Point Road. The ranch is located halfway between Job's Crossing and Center Point down a two-lane county road.

"This is where the property begins," Biggie said, pointing to a fence with steel posts.

"That's a mighty fine fence," Monica said. She was sitting on the jump seat between the front and back seats. "Lotsa money in that fence."

"New money," Mrs. Muckleroy said. "I remember when Old Man Barnwell didn't have a pot to, er . . ."

"... Cook his peas in." Miss Julia Lockhart said with a grin.

"How come it's so high?" I asked. "The fence, I mean."

"Oh, I expect they keep exotic animals in there." Monica craned her neck to see over the fence. "I saw a place over near Corsicana where they had a bunch of zebras and llamas and giraffes and stuff. See, you have to have a high fence so they can't jump out."

"You just know everything, don't you?" Sometimes Monica feels a need to show off.

"It's a deer fence," Rosebud said.

"You mean they keep deer? How come?" I asked.

"They don't keep them, J.R.," Biggie said. "They're trying to keep them out."

Miss Julia nodded her head. "That's right. The deer population has mushroomed out here in the last twenty years. Used to be, folks had to go 'way off to hunt. Now they say they practically come up in the yard and eat your shrubs."

"Turn here, Rosebud." Biggie pointed to a high gate with a sign over the top that said, BAR-LB RANCH.

The road wound for a quarter of a mile through green pastures surrounded by the same fence that bordered the road. Fat, Black Angus cattle grazed alongside sleek, brown horses. In a field by themselves, a small herd of Mexican goats grazed and twitched their short little tails. Occasionally, two kids would butt heads or playfully jump straight up into the air. We drove past two barns and a long bunkhouse before we pulled up in front of the main house.

"Lord, look at that place!" Mrs. Muckleroy put her hand over her mouth.

It was a long, low, Spanish-style ranch house made of stucco with a red tile roof. A deep veranda, supported by dark, rustic columns, ran all the way across the front of the building. Red, purple, and yellow flowers in hanging baskets and fat Mexican pots were everywhere.

"How in the world do they get that bougainvillea to grow this far north?" wondered Miss Julia.

Just then, the heavy oak doors were slung open, and one of the girls we had seen at the tearoom came out to greet us. I frowned as I remembered her being the one that had stuck her tongue out at me. She was dressed in the same blue shorts and white blouse she had worn before. She watched us without smiling as we piled out of the car and walked up the gravel path to the house.

"I'm Stacie," she said, beckoning with one pudgy hand, "Stacie Foxworth. I'm supposed to invite y'all in." She turned back toward the open front door talking over her shoulder. "I'm supposed to entertain you until the others get here, so y'all can just sit down anywhere you want to then I'll start the entertainment."

The living room was long and narrow with a huge, gray, stone fireplace against the back wall. Flanking the fireplace on either side were French doors through which we could see a fountain in the middle of an enclosed patio. Three saddle-colored leather sofas with Indian blankets slung over the backs were set at an angle in front of the hearth. A giant buffalo head looked down at us from above the mantle. He had a surprised expression on his face like he couldn't believe he had ended up like this.

The Mexican tile floor in front of the sofas was covered with a Navajo rug.

"Way cool," Monica breathed. "When I get a house, it's gonna be just like this."

Everybody took seats on the sofas. Biggie perched on the edge on account of her little legs are so short. "Well, Stacie," she said, "you must enjoy getting to spend the summer in a lovely place like this."

Stacie stood in front of the fireplace with her arms folded in front of her. "Huh? This place is a prison." She glared at Biggie.

"Oh, my." Miss Julia took a little notebook out of her purse and opened her fountain pen. "Tell us all about it, honey."

"Julia, put that up," Mrs. Muckleroy said. "We're guests here."

Miss Julia didn't put her notebook away, just kept looking at Stacie.

"How come you got that?" Stacie looked suspicious.

"She's a reporter for the paper," Monica said. "You better watch out what you say."

Biggie gave Monica a look. "Don't be sassy, young lady. And, Julia, Ruby's right. Put that thing away. Now, honey, what's on your mind?"

The girl, Stacie, looked at Miss Julia. "You're a real reporter? Are you going to print this?"

"Could be," Miss Julia said. Mrs. Muckleroy frowned.

The girl continued. "Well, for starters, we don't live in this big fine house. No way. We have to live in the bunkhouse, four to a room. And they make us make our own beds and wash our clothes—and on top of that they

56

don't hardly give us anything at all to eat."

"That doesn't sound too bad," Mrs. Muckleroy said. "After all, it's like a camp, isn't it? Why, I remember when Meredith Michelle went to scout camp, they had to sleep outside in a tent and actually cook their own food!" She took a handkerchief out of her purse and dabbed her forehead. "The poor child came home with her clothes all grass stained and muddy and her hair—well, I don't even want to think about it. I remember she literally *destroyed* a cute little tennis dress I bought from Neiman's. Well, you can imagine, I paid a pretty penny for that! Bless her heart, the whole experience just traumatized her. Now that's what I call roughing it."

"Ruby, you don't know anything." Miss Julia was miffed. "Why would you send clothes like that to a Girl Scout camp?"

"Oh, it's a whole lot worse here." Stacie wasn't going to let Mrs. Muckleroy steal her thunder. "They make us hike five miles every single day, rain or shine. And we have to get up at six o'clock every single day—even Sunday. I hate it, and as soon as I get out of here, I'm turning them in to the juvenile authorities. Child abuse is what I call it. I'm calling Mike Wallace, too."

"Stacie!"

We all looked around to see who had spoken. My mouth fell open. It was a girl standing in the doorway. She was dressed in the same blue-and-white uniform Stacie wore. But she wasn't carrying one single extra pound on her perfect little body. She had long hair, light brown, and it fell in tight ringlets all around her face, which was tanned a golden brown. Her eyes were big and bright blue green, the color of turquoise. She had long legs and a waist I could reach around with only my hands. My whole body turned to jelly, and I couldn't take my eyes off of her.

"What?" Stacie looked defiantly at the girl. "What am I doing? I was told to entertain the company so that's what I'm doing."

"No, you weren't," said the girl. "And Miss Higgins wants you back at the bunkhouse right now. You didn't finish mucking out the stalls this morning."

"See." Stacie looked at Mrs. Muckleroy. "We have to clean *stalls*. I'll bet your precious daughter didn't have to do that at camp!"

"Stacie, Laura's going to be disappointed in you."

Stacie stamped her foot. "I don't care what she thinks. I hate her!"

"Stacie, it's going to storm. Dad says we have to get the horses in the barn quick."

That seemed to do the trick. Stacie followed her out the door without another word.

I watched them leave, thinking how her voice sounded like music. Rosebud poked me with his elbow. "Shut your mouth before a fly gets in." He grinned at me.

6

Just then, a door opened at the far end of the room. "Welcome to Bar-LB." This was one of the women we had seen at the tearoom, the pretty one. She walked toward us. "I'm Laura Barnwell, director of the camp."

Biggie stood up and took a step toward her. "I'm Biggie Weatherford," she said, "and this is Ruby Muckleroy."

Mrs. Muckleroy stuck out her hand, the one with the big diamond ring. "So pleased," she said.

"And Julia Lockhart," Biggie said.

"You must be Rex's wife." Miss Julia never forgot she was a reporter.

Laura nodded with a smile before greeting each of us, ending with me and Monica. The lady shook hands and said something nice to every one of us.

"We'll have tea in the dining room," she said. "I believe it's ready, if you'd like to follow me."

"I reckon I'll pass," Rosebud said. "Okay if I look around outside?"

"Of course, if that's what you'd rather do," Laura said. "Make yourself at home. I think you'll find Hamp Caldwell, our combination vet and horse trainer, in the barn. I'm sure he'll be happy to show you around."

Rosebud went out one of the French doors while we followed Laura into the wood-paneled dining room.

Monica walked over and started examining the display of food piled on a sideboard along one wall. "Get back here," I hissed. Naturally, she ignored me.

Several people sat in tall-backed chairs with cowhide seats around a long ranch table under a deer-horn chandelier. Windows that reached from floor to ceiling showed a view of rolling hills dotted here and there with the same black cattle we had seen when we arrived.

Biggie looked at the windows with a worried frown. "Storm's coming—and it looks like a bad one."

Sure enough, black clouds boiled up from the tops of the distant woods.

"Tornado season," said a burly man, standing behind a chair at the end of the table. "Hamp's putting the horses in right now."

Laura spoke in a soft voice, but she somehow managed to get everyone's attention. "Everybody, allow me to present our honored guests from town." After she gave our names, she began to introduce the people around the table. She gestured toward a girl with short, black hair who looked to be in her twenties. "This is Rex's daughter, Babe."

Babe waved three fingers in our direction and looked at us with sparkling eyes. "Hey, everybody. Glad y'all could come." She bit into a baby cream puff. "Grab a plate and chow down."

"And this," Laura continued, "is Babe's husband, Rob Parish." She indicated a skinny guy. His thin, straight hair kept falling down over his eyes.

He brushed the hair back with his hand and nodded to us. "Gladameecha," was all he said.

"And this," Laura smiled, "the fellow with the weather report, is Abner Putnam, Rex's oldest friend and ranch foreman."

The burly man nodded and waved his hand toward the sideboard. "Y'all help yourselves, why doncha? We've got iced tea and coffee. Nobody around here drinks their tea hot."

We all moved toward the sideboard, which was piled with food that was anything but dietetic. I saw a pyramid of tiny cream puffs like the one Babe had been eating, just oozing with flavored whipped cream, a silver tray covered with cupcakes, little bitty tea sandwiches, and three or four pies. At one end stood a silver coffee pot and a crystal pitcher of iced tea.

Mrs. Muckleroy, loading up her plate, couldn't hold back any longer. "Where's Rex?" she asked, looking over her shoulder.

"He begged to be excused. But Grace Higgins, our dietitian, should be here any minute. I can't imagine why she's late," Laura said.

"I hope he's not ill." Mrs. Muckleroy wouldn't let it go. She glanced at Biggie out of the corner of her eye.

"Shut up, Ruby," Miss Julia muttered.

"Oh, Daddy's always ill," Babe said. "He's got aches and pains he hasn't even used yet." Her voice sounded bitter.

"Ah, here's Grace." Laura Barnwell passed around a plate of coconut macaroons. "Come on in, Grace, so I can introduce you."

It was the other lady we'd seen at the tearoom. Today, she was dressed in Eastern-style riding britches with brown boots. She wore a white Polo shirt, open at the neck. "Trouble in the ranks," she muttered, as she passed Laura. "I may need your help."

"Later." Laura seemed unfazed.

Just then, the doorbell rang and Abner left to answer it. I got up to refill my plate. From the sideboard, I could see the front hall. A strong gust of wind blew in as Abner opened the door to let in a blond man wearing a blue suit. He put his briefcase on a hall table and followed Abner into the dining room.

"Why Jeremy!" Laura looked startled. "What brings you here? And in this weather, too."

The man walked over and kissed her on the cheek. "Laura, pretty as ever. Hon, I have to talk to Rex. It can't be handled over the phone. May I spend the night?"

"Of course." Laura flashed a look at Grace. "Nothing's wrong, I hope?"

"I hope not. I'll discuss it with Rex tonight."

"Then have some tea with us. Rex is resting."

Biggie stirred sugar into her tea then turned to Laura. "So tell us about your program here. It sounds intriguing."

"Oh, Lord, don't get her started." Babe rolled her eyes.

"No, we'd all like to know," Miss Julia said, taking out her pad and pencil.

"Well, if you insist." Laura began to talk, and anyone could tell she was awfully excited about what they were doing. "Let me start by telling you *why* I decided to open a camp for overweight girls," she said. "It stems from my own past. I was brought up in Tyler, the oldest of four girls. My father was not the wealthiest man in town, but he was successful in the oil business and was active in many civic and charitable causes. As a result of that, three of us girls were asked to participate in the Queen's Court at the Rose Festival. My sister was chosen queen. Are you all aware of what that means?"

"Of course," Mrs. Muckleroy piped up. "That's the most prestigious event in the city. Only girls from the finest families are asked to be duchesses. And to be selected queen, well . . ."

"It means you have to be rich enough to afford the pageant dress!" Babe bit into a cookie. "Let alone all the outfits you have to buy for all the parties."

Laura ignored her. "My younger sister, Ellen, was the sweetest, most loving girl you could ever hope to meet, and the smartest, too. And funny? She was a natural mimic and could do impressions of everyone we knew." She looked at Biggie. "But never in a mean way, if you know what I mean. She just observed people and had a pure talent for picking up on their mannerisms. She wanted to become an actress, and we were all convinced she could become a big star."

63

"She was a natural," Miss Julia commented.

"Exactly." Laura nodded her head. "Ellen was smart, too. She graduated top of her class in high school. Everyone thought she'd go far in life. In her junior year, she sent applications to several colleges, and it looked like she could take her choice. They all wanted her."

"She must have been the sister who was chosen queen," Mrs. Muckleroy said.

"No, that was Beth. Ellen was never asked. In the week of spring break, before her high school graduation, mother decided to take Ellen on a trip up East to look over some of the schools. My sisters and I went along for the fun of it." She folded her napkin and placed it beside her plate. "We flew into Logan Airport in Boston and rented a car. New England is beautiful in the spring, and we were all in a festive mood. We looked forward to visiting the various campuses and helping Ellen select just the right one." She looked out the window and continued to talk just as if she was reliving that trip. "The first school we visited was an exclusive girls' college. In their letter, they had seemed the most interested in having her. The campus was covered with cherry trees, just dripping blossoms all over the walkways that led from one ivy-covered building to the next. And the girls, they all looked happy and content to be there. Mother suggested that we visit the dean of students, just to get acquainted, you see." All of a sudden, a big tear rolled out of her eye. She blotted it away with her napkin.

Grace, the dietitian, put her hand over Laura's. "You don't have to tell this." Her voice was brusque. "It always makes you cry."

"But I do, Grace. Don't you see? People need to un-derstand—they have to!" She turned back to Biggie, who was listening with a little frown on her face. "The trip was lovely. We visited four schools and were greeted warmly at each one. After that, we visited Martha's Vine-yard and Nantucket. We drove up through New Hamp-shire and Maine. We ate our fill of Maine lobster and clam chowder, shopped at L.L.Bean, explored some lovely New England villages, then boarded our plane back to Texas satisfied that our trip had been a rousing success."

"Which school did she choose?" Mrs. Muckleroy asked.

"None of them. Something happened that made her decide to stay home."

"For heaven's sake, what?" Miss Julia wanted to know.

"Some of the other girls in her high school became jealous of her—because she was going East to school, you see. They began writing nasty notes and putting them in her desk at school. They started a rumor she was preg-nant—by the school janitor! And you know kids; they believed it. The rest of her senior year was a living hell. My dear sweet Ellen became so depressed, Mama had to have her committed to a mental hospital."

"But why—why would they do that?"

"Because she was FAT!" Monica bit into her fourth cream puff.

Biggie looked daggers at Monica. "Was that it?" she asked Laura.

Laura nodded, wiping away another tear. "She was the only one of us girls who had a weight problem. She took after two of our aunts on my father's side. It wasn't her fault—it was genetic, don't you see? Ellen wasn't even a heavy eater. She just metabolized her food differently—and she was so sweet and funny, we never even thought about her weight until that happened. Then we knew we couldn't ignore it any longer. She was sick because of her size; it was as plain as day."

"I'm sure glad I don't have that problem," Babe said. "I never gain an ounce no matter how much I eat." She got up from the table and started reloading her plate just to prove it.

"Just wait until you hit forty." Grace glared at her.

Babe stuck out her tongue at Grace.

"So what happened to Ellen?" I asked. "Did she ever get to be an actress?"

"No. When she came out of the hospital, she was changed. All the spark had gone out of her. She didn't seem to care about anything anymore, and within a year, she weighed over four hundred pounds. The family was worried and urged her to look for a job in Tyler where we could look after her."

"Nobody would hire her I bet." Monica is my friend, but she has a smart mouth on her.

"That's right. She couldn't find work. She went to the community college for a semester and lived at home with Mama and Daddy. In her spare time, she would help out down at the little theater, painting sets and being stage manager, stuff like that. They never seemed to have a part for someone her size. By that time I had married my first husband and had a home of my own in Tyler. We used to go out to lunch from time to time. By then Ellen had lost her sunny nature. She hardly ever did impressions anymore or told jokes. We all missed her infectious laugh. Then two things happened. The first was, Ellen got a job. Oh, it wasn't much of one. She worked in the stockroom of one of those giant office supply stores. She spent all day loading heavy cartons onto shelves and pushing furniture around." Laura paused, thinking. "She seemed happy, though, making her own money for the first time. She even lost a few pounds. Then one day the store held what they called a Review Day. That's when the big shots from the regional office would visit to grade the store's efficiency. Ellen was behind a stack of heavy boxes working away when she heard one of the inspectors talking to the assistant manager. He said, 'Get that fat heifer out of here before she falls down and we have a lawsuit on our hands.' Poor Ellen got her purse and walked right out of there without even turning in her resignation."

"I can't believe it. How cruel." Miss Julia was incensed.

"What was the second thing that happened?" Monica wanted to know.

"The second thing was, she fell in love."

"Sad," Mrs. Muckleroy murmured.

"Yes, it was. She fell for the executive director of the theater group. We never knew why. He was a little, stooped-over man who had sparse hair and wore wire-rimmed glasses. I guess it was their mutual passion for theater that attracted her. Naturally, she never said anything to a living soul—except me that is. But somehow, the others found out. Ellen wore her heart on her sleeve."

"I can relate," Mrs. Muckleroy said. "I wear my heart on my sleeve, too. Don't I, Biggie?"

"I guess," Biggie said. "Did the others tease her or something?"

"Unmercifully. Theater people can be quite cruel without even knowing it. I think it's because they're both creative and maybe just a bit self-involved."

Jeremy Polk had been listening intently. "Now, Laura, that's a pretty broad generalization."

"Spoken like a lawyer," Grace said. "Can't you see why Laura might be just a little one-sided on this? You've heard this story, Jere."

"Right. Sorry, Laura."

"One night," Laura continued, "Ellen went in for a late rehearsal and found the cast putting on an im-promptu skit about her and the man. It ended with the fellow running for his life while the actress who played my sister, arms outstretched, tripped over a stool and fell flat on her face trying to catch him. Ellen, tears streaming down her face, ran from the theater to the sound of hoots and laughter."

"That was mean," Monica said.

"She went to my parents' house, took my daddy's pistol out of the drawer beside his bed, and took it back to her apartment." Laura spoke in a flat voice like she had told this story a hundred times. "Ellen lay down on her bed and shot herself in the head. She left a note. It said, 'Don't grieve for me. I'm happy to leave this hideous shell of a body. I love you all. Tonight I shall fly with the angels.' " Laura hung her head. "My baby sister didn't need to die like that. At her funeral I promised myself that I would do everything in my power to protect other young girls from the heartache Ellen had to suffer."

"But how could you do that?" Biggie asked. "You said her weight problem was genetic."

Laura drew herself up tall and sighed. "That's where Grace comes in," she said, her face beginning to lighten up. "Tell them, Grace."

7

Grace leaned her elbows on the table, folding her little square hands in front of her. "I graduated from Texas A&M with a degree in food service and nutrition. My plans were to go into the restaurant business—maybe become a chef someday. A friend of mine who was going into the Peace Corps urged me to join her. 'It's a chance to have a little adventure and see the world,' she kept saying. 'You're going to be working all your life. Have a little fun first.' Well, she didn't know what she was talking about." Grace smiled at her plate. "Anne didn't last a month in the Peace Corps, which turned out to be really hard work with substandard living conditions. I, on the other hand, enjoyed the challenge."

"Where did you go?" Miss Julia asked.

"The Co-operative Republic of Guyana. I ended up

going with a team that was assigned to teach modern farming methods to the Indians."

"Where is Guyana?" Monica crumbled a cookie on her plate.

"It's in Africa, darling," Mrs. Muckleroy said smugly.

Grace smiled. "A lot of people think that. Actually, it's in South America. It's between Venezuela, Suriname, and Brazil, and on its northern coast there's the Atlantic Ocean. The country is not very big, but there are miles and miles of unspoiled tropical rainforest and a large savanna—that's grasslands. You should see the Kaieteur Falls. They are immense—and surrounded by trees and wildlife."

"What kind of wildlife?" I wanted to know.

"Oh, many different kinds of monkeys, ocelots, and parrots. They have tapirs there, too, but they are shy and don't show themselves much."

"Get to the diet, hon," Laura said. "I just love that part."

"I will, I will. I just want to fill in a little background first." She took a sip of tea then continued. "I arrived in Georgetown by air, then took a small plane to the Rupununi Savanna where we were to settle in an Amerindian village. It was in February, right after the rainy season. Boy, was it hot! We were greeted warmly by the people and shown to two small huts, which were to be our homes for a whole year. We cooked our food over a wood fire and brought up water from a nearby stream—there are many streams crisscrossing the savanna."

"Ugh. How could you stand it?" Mrs. Muckleroy said.

"Oh, you get used to it. It was the heat that was the worst—that and the insects. We had to check our beds every night for scorpions and other vermin. And we had to boil our drinking water. There's always the threat of cholera, you know."

Abner Putnam scraped his chair back and went to stand by the window. I looked and saw that the clouds were getting blacker. The wind had died so not a leaf moved on the two mimosa trees in the backyard. "Think I'll see if everything is taken care of out there," he said, heading for the door.

Jeremy got up, too. "I'm going to see if Rex is up and about," he said.

Laura waved them out of the room. "Go on, Grace."

"Actually," Grace said "their diets were not bad; they relied heavily on seafood and fresh fruit from the forests. They make a spicy stew from fish and thicken it with cassava juice."

"What's that?" I asked.

"Cassava? It's a plant that has a tuberous root, like a potato. Do you ever eat tapioca?"

"Not any more than I have to," Monica put in.

"They have it in the school cafeteria. Yuk," I said.

"Well, tapioca comes from the cassava plant. The Indians used other plants from the savanna—things we in our country are unaware of. That's where I got the diet."

"Why would they need a diet?" Biggie looked skeptical. "I've watched lots of nature shows—and I've never seen a fat Indian."

"You're right," Grace said. "It's the civilized world that overindulges on food. Indigenous folks rarely do.

72

The person who needed to diet was Sammy Spratt, a member of our own team. The poor guy was so overweight that he suffered something awful from the heat and the rigors of life down there. Frankly, I don't know how he ever passed the Peace Corps physical. Who knows? Anyway, things got so bad Sammy was afraid he was going to have to give up and go home—and he really didn't want to do that. The villagers laughed like crazy when he came around. They had never in their lives seen a fat person."

"Poor old Sammy," Monica said.

"Well, you can say this for Sammy, he was a trooper," Grace said. "He was determined not to give up even though he had heat rash in every fold of his body, and he huffed and puffed at the slightest bit of exertion.

"One day I was showing some of the women how to make a salad from some of the native greens. Sammy walked by and they began to titter behind their hands as usual. One of the women, Arawa, asked me why he was so fat. I couldn't tell her. 'I can make him thin,' said the oldest woman in the group. The others laughed and nodded their heads. When I asked her to explain, she said not to worry, that she would brew up a potion that would make him thin in a matter of weeks."

Grace smiled, remembering. "I promptly forgot about it until a week later when I saw that Sammy was noticeably thinner. When I remarked on it, he looked embarrassed but confessed that Mea, the old woman, had been bringing him the potion to drink every night at bedtime. He said he had never felt better in his life. I'll admit, I was concerned. What if she was giving him strong emet-

73

ics or diuretics that might damage his health? He said no—that his body functions had not been affected."

"And he kept on losing weight?" Biggie asked. "Without going on any diet?"

"That's right. Not only that, his skin tone improved as well as his eyesight and hearing. He felt wonderful! Within the month, he was down to his ideal weight and feeling even better. I asked the old woman to give me the formula for the potion. I wrote it down, put it in my footlocker, and just left it there. We were so busy with other things."

Just then, Jeremy came back into the room. "Rex wants to rest until three," he said.

"Fine." Laura pushed her chair back and got to her feet. "Suppose we all retire to the living room where we can be more comfortable. Then, if you're interested, I'll tell you the rest of the story."

As it happened, we had to wait awhile before we heard any more. Just as we all got seated in the big living room, the storm hit. A noise like a supersonic jet flying low passed overhead, and all the lights went out. An instant later we heard a sound like an explosion in the distance. The mimosa trees, which had been so still before, were bent almost to the ground. I looked out the window just in time to see a wooden bucket go tumbling across the yard followed by what looked like a piece off the bunkhouse. Next came a round hay bale. As it rolled along, hunks of straw came loose and rose straight up into the sky like helium balloons.

I heard a woman scream, Mrs. Muckleroy I think. Grace Higgins held Laura's hand, while Miss Julia ran to the window to see what was happening. For a second I was frozen on the spot, then Jeremy Polk took charge.

"Everybody move to an inside wall. Hurry!" He grabbed Miss Julia by the arm and pulled her into the middle of the room. "Those windows could implode any second now."

Without a word, we all moved away from the windows and stood in a row like ducks against the back wall waiting to see what was going to happen next. Biggie stood between me and Monica, her arms around each of us. I looked up at the swaying chandelier, wondering whether the roof would hold.

It was over as suddenly as it had started. And the quiet was heavy and damp. Now a steady rain fell outside the window. Dumbly, we looked at one another and moved to our seats around the fireplace. In a few minutes, the door burst open, and Abner Putnam rushed in.

"Is everyone okay?" He was bareheaded and dripping wet.

Grace had taken a seat next to Laura, still holding her hand. Laura looked scared to death. She put her hand to her breast. "Tell me quickly, are the girls all right?"

"The girls are fine," he said. "No damage at all. The tornado missed us by a half mile." He sat on the edge of a chair. "I saw the funnel—between here and town. I watched it come on down out of the clouds. Law me, what a sight! Then when the tail touched down, man I saw whole trees picked up and tossed around like goddamn toothpicks." He picked up a magazine and commenced fanning himself with it.

Laura took a deep breath. "The horses. Are they all right?"

"We got them in just in time." He looked at Biggie. "Rosebud was a big help."

"What about your cows?" Monica asked.

"Cows know what to do in a storm," he replied. "Most of them went down in a dry creek bed and turned their backs to the wind." He looked at Laura. "We did lose a couple of calves, though."

"Sounds like you were mighty lucky," Biggie said. "I wonder how the rest of the county is faring. Do you have any word from town?"

"Oh, my goodness!" Mrs. Muckleroy gasped. "Do you think that thing went through town?"

"Sorry. Don't have a clue. Well, I'd better get out there and crank up the auxiliary generator." He turned at the door. "Folks, thank your lucky stars. We've been mighty fortunate today."

Suddenly, Laura jumped to her feet. "My God, poor Rex. I'd better go see about him." She hurried from the room.

"Is he bedridden?" Biggie asked Grace.

"Oh, heavens no. But he does tire easily, what with the diabetes and having his leg amputated. Sometimes he uses a wheelchair—other times, just a walker."

I heard the front door open and saw Rosebud come striding in. "Miss Biggie, I've had the car radio on. They sayin' the storm just barely missed town."

"What a relief." Biggie sat down with a plop.

"Thank God in heaven!" Mrs. Muckleroy said. "If it got my hundred-year-old magnolia, I'd just about die."

"If it got your tree, it'ud probably get your house, too." Monica smarted off.

"Oh, Lordy, I guess you're right," Mrs. Muckleroy said weakly. She took out a hankie and patted her brow.

"Well, you see, what I mean to say is, it didn't go right through town. It done right smart of damage out on the bypass. Taken out that there Fresh-As-a-Daisy café and the Big Eight Motel, wellsir, the radio says it got plumb flattened."

"Wow! That's close to our house!" My heart turned over. "Rosebud, what about Willie Mae?"

"She's okay, I reckon." Rosebud didn't sound so sure. "They said no houses were destroyed."

"We've got to get home right now." Biggie got up and started toward Rosebud.

"Come on!" Miss Julia grabbed her purse off a table.

"Wellum, we can't do that." Rosebud shook his head.

"Why?" Biggie wanted to know.

"On account of there's trees down all over the road between here and there. They're sending out crews with chain saws to get them clear." Rosebud looked down at Biggie. "But, Miss Biggie, we ain't gonna get home before morning."

I had never seen Biggie look so scared.

Just then the lights came back on.

Laura came back into the room. "Rex is okay. Grace, will you see to the girls? They must be petrified." She turned at the doorway. "Now you all just make your-selves at home. Feel free to tour the house if you like. Since you'll be staying the night, I'll tell Josefina to get your rooms ready. We'll have supper at seven."

77

"Come on, Ruby," said Miss Julia. "I've been dying to see the rest of this house."

Rosebud spoke to Biggie. "I'd better go back out and help them fellers down at the barn."

"By all means," Biggie said.

"I'll help," Monica said and followed Rosebud out the door.

After they left the rest of us got comfortable around the fireplace. Biggie sat on a low chair next to Jeremy Polk and crossed her little feet in front of her.

"Well, Mr. Polk," she said, "you sure know how to take charge in an emergency. I'll bet you've had some kind of training in that sort of thing."

"I used to be in the National Guard, Miss, uh, Biggie, is it?"

"I'm afraid that's it," Biggie said. "My real name is Fiona Wooten Weatherford, but most people just call me Biggie. You see, when J.R. was small his daddy wanted him to call me Big Mama, but he had a hard time saying that, so he ended up calling me Biggie and the name stuck." She smiled. "Are you a lawyer, Mr. Polk?" She looked at the briefcase on the floor next to his chair.

"That's right. I've been representing Rex Barnwell since my father retired. He was Uncle Rex's lawyer before that."

"Uncle Rex? Are you related then?"

"Oh, no, ma'am. It's just, I've known him all my life. Dad and he were lifelong friends."

"Oh?" Biggie tucked one foot under her knee and leaned forward. I could tell she was settling in for a long chat. "I've known Rex for a long time, too."

"So I understand," he said.

"Are you by any chance related to Hiram and Geneva Polk from Center Point?" Biggie asked.

"As a matter of fact, I am. Hiram was my great uncle."

"What a small world it is," Biggie said. "Geneva Polk was my mother's third cousin on her father's side. I guess that makes us kissing cousins."

Jeremy's face brightened. "Miss Biggie, lately I've become interested in genealogy. I'm very anxious to find out something about the Kemp County branch of my family. Do you think you could help me with that?"

Biggie grinned from ear to ear. "I expect so," she said. "Genealogy happens to be one of my specialties. I'm the president of the James Royce Wooten chapter of the Daughters of the Republic of Texas and former recording secretary for our local DAR chapter. It just happens that I have a great deal of material on your family in my file at home."

"Wonderful!" Jeremy took a business card out of his pocket and handed it to Biggie. "I'd be grateful for any information you could send me. You'll be reimbursed for postage, of course." He glanced at his watch and picked up his briefcase. "Look at the time. Will you excuse me, Miss Biggie? I really need to go over these papers before I present them to Rex." He stood up. "It's been very nice chatting with you."

Before Biggie could answer, Laura came back into the room. "Jeremy, Rex says he'll see you after supper. Right now, Miss Biggie, he'd really like a short visit with you."

8

Biggie got to her feet.

"You want me to come, Biggie?" I was surprised to find I was curious about my real granddaddy.

"Not just now," she said. "I may send for you later."

I picked up a magazine and thumbed through it. It was all about raising cattle, a subject I'm not much interested in. The sun had come out now, and except for the tree limbs all over the yard, you would never know we'd just had a bad storm. I got up and looked through the French door and went outside onto a stone patio with a fountain in the middle. I looked around and saw that the house was built in a "U" shape around this patio, with four sets of French doors opening into different rooms. Trumpet vines grew over the walls and snaked around the doors. I walked across the patio and looked at the grassy slope of the yard. To my right stood the barn and bunkhouse and beyond them, behind board fences, the cattle and goats grazed. Rosebud was standing beside one fence talking to a man wearing a cowboy hat. I headed in their direction but before I got there, Monica called my name.

"Hey, J.R. Over here," she said. "I want you to meet my new friend."

She was standing just inside the barn. Next to her stood the girl I'd seen earlier, the one who had come for Stacie. Monica didn't seem to notice I'd turned red all over. "This is Misty, Misty Caldwell. Her dad's a vet. He works here all the time taking care of the animals. Misty, this is J.R. He's kind of dorky, but he's my best friend anyway." She waited for me to give her a shove like I always do when she says something smart like that.

All I could get out of my mouth was, "Pleased to meet you."

Misty put out her hand. I've never shaken hands with a girl before, but I put mine out and awkwardly squeezed her hand. She laughed. "Don't pay any attention to Monica. She's been telling me real nice things about you. She says you're the bravest boy she knows."

"And we've been through some tight spots together. Right, J.R.?" Monica waited for me to start in bragging, but I couldn't.

"I guess," I said.

"Would you like to help us groom the horses?" Misty asked. "Dad says we need to give them lots of attention to gentle them down after the storm."

"Sure!"

I followed them into the barn. It was cool and smelled

81

like fresh hay and feed and damp dirt. Six horses stood in stalls lined up against one side. They whinnied and stamped their feet when they saw Misty. Misty handed me a brush and led me to a big roan standing in the first stall. "You can start with Star. He's gentle and good with strangers. Just pat him and stroke him. After he gets to know you a little, just brush in the direction the hair grows. Like this." She put her hand over mine to show me how. Her hand was tiny and soft.

Monica made a face at me over the horse's back. "You don't have to show me. I already know how." She grabbed a brush off the shelf and started brushing the horse in the next stall.

"Yeah, right," I said. "That's because you spend so much time grooming that old mule your daddy's got."

While we worked, Misty went to a barrel in the corner of the barn, scooped out a bucket of feed, and brought it to feed the horses. "You can't feed them too much, they'll get colic." She stroked the horse's head and talked softly to him while he ate.

"Yeah," Monica said. "A horse will keep on eating 'til its stomach busts. My daddy told me that."

Monica can be the world's biggest know-it-all at times. But I didn't say anything, just kept brushing and listening to her brag about how much she knows about horses.

After we finished the grooming and feeding, Misty led us into the tack room and opened a little refrigerator. "Y'all want a cold drink?"

We nodded. While Misty got the drinks, I looked around the little room. The only light came from a small window set high on one wall. Under it, next to a shelf piled with saddle blankets, a pegboard held bridles, ropes, and other tack. Along the solid wall to the right, six odd-looking black saddles hung in a row.

I walked over and touched one. "What kind of saddles are these?" I asked.

Misty handed me a Big Red. "They're English saddles."

"They're just flat like that? Where's the horn? And the seat?"

Misty laughed. "My daddy uses a western saddle, but the girls all use these."

"I know all about English saddles," Monica bragged. "I saw *National Velvet* on TV just the other night." She turned to Misty. "J.R. doesn't know much about this stuff."

I chose to ignore that remark.

"Let's sit down," Misty said.

She led us to a spot in the corner, and we sat down on bags of oats. I sat next to Misty, while Monica plopped herself down across the room.

"How do you like living here?" I asked Misty.

"It's okay," she said, "since I don't have to be part of the program."

"Well." I looked at her. "You sure don't need to be on any diet."

"Thanks," she said. "I've never had to worry about my weight."

"Your hair's pretty, too."

"So's yours. I just love guys with brown hair and blue eyes. Just like Tom Cruise."

I was embarrassed and didn't know what to say. No girl had ever given me a compliment before. "Well, uh . . ."

Then Monica spoke up. "Hey, J.R., how come your ears are so red? Bee sting you or something?" With that, she laughed way too loud and went out the door, slamming it behind her.

Misty just smiled and looked down at her hands clasped together in her lap. I thought she was the most beautiful thing I had ever seen in my life, and I would have been plenty happy to just sit there with her all afternoon. But I heard Rosebud's footsteps crunching on the gravel path outside.

"J.R., you in there?"

"Here."

He came and stood at the door. "Miss Biggie says for you to come to the house. Mr. Rex wants to see you."

I said good-bye to Misty and followed Rosebud out of the barn and into the bright sunlight.

"You go on up to the house," Rosebud said. "I'm gonna help these fellers clear up out here."

I looked around me before starting up the path to the house. About fifty yards from the barn, I saw a large riding ring with jumping hazards set up on both sides. Around the outside edge of the ring, someone had built a cinder track. The girls were doing laps around it, with Stacie holding up the rear. Even from that distance, I could hear her whining and complaining. Grace Higgins stood on the sidelines looking at what I guessed must be a stopwatch.

Biggie was standing outside the door waiting for me when I got to the house.

"He wants to meet you," she said.

"Did you tell him? Everything?"

"That you're his grandson? Of course, J.R. He has a right to know."

I followed her through the living and dining rooms, down a wide hallway paved with Spanish tiles. She tapped on a door, opened it, and went in. I followed.

The room was large and bright with wood paneling on all four walls. A king-sized bed angled out from the corner, and next to it French doors opened to the patio. A lot of medicine bottles stood on the mantel that hung over a big, empty fireplace. Rex Barnwell was in a leather armchair next to the fireplace. Even though his body looked small in that large chair, his shoulders were broad and he had big hands and feet. I figured he must have been a mighty big man in his day. He motioned to me to come toward him.

"Why, Fiona, he looks just like you—except maybe a little like me as a boy." He kept staring at me until I squirmed. Then he laughed—a big, hearty laugh. "Sorry, son. I didn't mean to embarrass you. Have a seat on that stool over there so I can look at you. Your granny tells me this is all brand-new to you, getting a new grandpa you never knew you had. Well, it's new to me, too."

"I never heard anybody call her Fiona before." I nodded toward Biggie, who had taken a seat in a chair opposite Rex.

"No fooling? What do they call her?"

I explained to him about how I couldn't say Big Mama when I was little so I shortened it to Biggie. I told him how everybody in town calls her that now.

He laughed again. "Biggie, huh? Well, I say that doesn't fit worth a damn. She's no bigger than a gnat. Never was." He looked fondly at Biggie.

I looked at a picture of a car over the mantel. A man stood beside it wearing racing gear. "Is that you?"

The smile left his face. "It was, son. It was. Would you like to have that picture?"

"I sure would!"

"Then take it home with you when you go. Now I want you to tell me all about yourself. Fill me in on all the time I've missed."

I didn't know where to start, so I just started at the first. "I was born in Dallas," I said. "That's where my mama and daddy lived a long time ago. Daddy was in business for himself."

"Don't say. And what was that?"

"He rented out Porta Potties."

"Porta Potties, huh? Any money in that?"

"I guess. I was only six when he died. Then I came to live with Biggie."

"What happened to your mama?"

"Oh, she didn't much want me, I guess. She's the nervous type. Anyway, I'd rather live with Biggie in Job's Crossing than in Dallas."

"Can't say I blame you for that. Now, Biggie, about the will. I'm going to have Jeremy . . ."

Just then there was a knock on the door and Laura came in. She smiled at me and Biggie. "I'm sorry to interrupt," she said, "but Dr. Beall is here to see you."

Biggie stood up. "We'll go. I want to see the barns before dark."

"Wait," Rex said. "Don't forget to take your picture," he said to me. He turned to Laura. "Honey, I've given that picture to J.R. Can you take it down for him?"

"Of course." Laura took the picture from the mantel and handed it to me. "He was a handsome man, wasn't he?"

I looked closer. He was tanned and rugged looking, with curly black hair that hung down over his forehead. He had blue eyes the same color as mine. "Yes'm. He sure was."

We turned to go.

"Wait," Rex said. "Fiona, will I see you tomorrow? Please. I have a lot more to talk over with you."

"You have your doctor's appointment early tomorrow morning. Have you forgotten?" Laura kissed him on top of his bald head.

"And we have to be getting back to town as soon as the road is cleared," Biggie said.

"Then come back Friday." He begged Biggie with his eyes.

"Yes, please. Come for dinner," Laura said. "This poor darling man has little enough to brighten his life. By all means, come."

"I suppose we could do that," Biggie started toward the door. "Do you know where Julia and Ruby are?"

"They went to their rooms for a little rest before supper."

"Then I'll do the same."

9

After leaving the picture in my room, I followed my nose to the backyard. Somewhere, someone was cooking barbecue, and I aimed to find it. Sure enough, I found Rosebud and Abner Putnam standing beside a giant brick pit next to a grove of pines between the house and barn. Redwood picnic tables stood in a row under the trees. A fifty-gallon drum held ice and cans of soda and beer. Rosebud, with a beer in one hand, turned the sizzling chicken halves with the long fork he had in his other hand.

"Hey," I said.

"Hey yourself. Where's Miss Biggie?"

"Resting in her room. We having barbecue for supper?"

Rosebud cocked his head at me.

"Well, I was just asking. Golly."

"What do it look like we havin'?"

Abner came and laid a hand on my shoulder. "Don't mind him, son. How 'bout getting me a beer." He tossed his empty can in a plastic trash bin.

"Can I have a Big Red?"

"You betcha," Abner said. "Soon as you take this pan in and tell Josefina to fill her up with more mopping sauce."

I got the beer for Abner and headed back toward the house with the empty pan. Then I realized I didn't know where I was going. "Where's the kitchen?"

Abner pointed to a door at the far end of the house half-hidden by a large magnolia tree. I knocked on the door. Someone was singing inside. Suddenly the door opened and a little bitty Mexican lady stood looking at me. She was dressed in a blue Mexican dress with bright embroidery around the neck. "And who are you?" she asked.

I told her who I was. "Abner sent me in for more sauce."

"So, the lazy man can't walk a few steps for more sauce and has to send our guest to do his job. Well, come in, *muchachito.* How would you like a piece of pie while he waits for the sauce?"

"I better get back. He might need it now."

"Lemonade then?"

"I've got a Big Red waiting for me." I handed her the pan.

"So, the macho man needs you back. Here, then." She took the pan and filled it with good smelling sauce from a pot on the stove. "Careful now, it is very hot."

"I'll see you later," I said from the door.

"You surely will," she said.

I got my Big Red and stood around listening while Rosebud and Abner cooked barbecue and talked.

"Yeah, I've been with Rex since his racing days," Abner said. "I lost me own leg in a wreck at Indy in '53." He raised up his jeans a little and rapped twice on a shiny, pink, plastic shin. " 'Course, I couldn't drive any more, so Rex took me on as his crew boss."

"How do you get a cowboy boot on that thing?" I asked.

"It's built right onto my wooden leg," Abner said. He pulled on the boot and it didn't budge. "See here, the thing won't come off for nothin'."

"What'll you do when those boots wear out?" They looked pretty run down to me.

Abner scratched his head and looked up at the sky. "Wellsir, reckon I'll go back to the feller that made this leg and have a new one put on. If I live that long, that is. These here boots got plenty of miles left on 'um.

"Now, like I was saying about old Rex, he designed the very first fiberglass racing helmet. I forget who was the first to test it out. One of them Unsers maybe? Naw, it was before them. Anyway, now all of them guys wear that same helmet. That Rex, he's really something."

"Uh-huh." Rosebud took a long string of sausages out of a red cooler. "Ready to put these on?"

Abner nodded. "Yep, old Rex, he's the best. Nerve like a cougar, don't you know, and smart, too. You ever hear about the car he designed? The Baracuda? Best in its class in its day. Won I don't know how many awards for design excellence."

He went on like that until the sausages were done and the chickens were piled up in a big roaster pan. All Rosebud had to do was throw in an Un-HUH from time to time and sip on his beer.

I was getting hungry. "What time are we eating?"

"Right soon," Abner said. "Here comes Josefina with the fixings now."

As soon as we had the tables all set with tin plates and cups and red paper napkins and the food lined up on a long table made from two sawhorses and a hollow-core door, here came the girls, jogging down from the bunkhouse with Grace Higgins in the lead. Abner took an iron rod and rattled it against a triangle hanging from a tree branch to call the folks down from the big house. Soon we were all seated, Biggie on my right and Monica on my left.

"Where've you been?" I asked Monica.

"I'll tell you later," she said. "Shh, Grace is saying something."

"Everybody, quiet down." She turned to Biggie. "We say some words before meals, words of thanks to Nature and the Universe. Girls!"

The girls all rose to their feet and stretched their arms over their heads. Then they chanted something that I couldn't understand one single word of. It sounded a little like: Ummm-gallawatchitt-hoooooo. They said that three times then sat down and drank something out of half coconut shells before plowing into the food on the table.

I turned to Biggie. "What do you reckon that is?"

She didn't answer, just shook her head as if to say I should keep quiet about it.

The sun was setting red over the trees when we finished eating.

"Red sun at night, sailor's delight," Monica said. "It's gonna be a pretty day tomorrow, Miss Biggie."

"You're right," Biggie said. "How about the three of us taking a little walk while there's still some daylight?"

We walked around the corrals and through the barn, stopping to talk to the horses as they hung their heads over their stalls.

"Maybe I'll ask to have a ride tomorrow," Biggie said. "It's been a long time since I've sat a horse."

"Would you really, Miss Biggie?" Monica said. "I'd give a hundred dollar bill to see that."

"If you had it," I said.

"It was just a figure of speech. J.R., don't you know what a figure of speech is?"

"Yeah, right. Here's the back door." I pulled open the kitchen door and the others followed me in.

Josefina was standing at the sink wiping it out with a clean towel.

"Josefina, this is my grandmother, Biggie, and this is Monica Sontag." I hoped Biggie noticed I remembered my manners.

"*Hay, Madre de Dios,* and me looking such a mess." Josefina smoothed her salt-and-pepper hair. "Oh well, sit and have some hot chocolate with me. I've just taken Señor Rex's in to him."

We drank delicious hot chocolate out of Mexican

mugs while Biggie asked Josefina questions. She can't help it. It's just Biggie's nature to be as curious as a raccoon in a campground.

"Have you been with Mr. Rex long?"

"Me? Not Mr. Rex. I have been with Miss Laura almost all her life. You see, she was born in Monterrey, Mexico, my hometown. I came to the family when my Laura was a baby after her mother died in an automobile accident. Her father was a busy man and left her raising to me."

"And you've been with her ever since?" Monica's mouth dropped open.

"Oh no, *nina*. I was only a girl when I came to tend to Laura when she was born. Her parents were Anglos living in Mexico. Her father had cattle ranches and oil interests there." Josefina refilled our cocoa mugs then sat down at the table with us. "She was so beautiful with her golden ringlets and blue eyes. People would stop and stare and want to touch her when I took her out to the market. And charming! *Ay*, my baby never got into trouble. When she would steal money from her papa's wallet to buy trinkets at the market, her papa would try to be angry with her." She laughed. "But he never could. She would admit her sins in such a sweet and appealing manner that nobody could bear to punish her. And truly, she meant no harm. Most times, with tears in her eyes, she would give the trinkets to some poor child on the streets. She could not bear to see a single person in need. She would say to me, 'Mamá, why do we have so much when they have so little?' " Josefina smiled at the memory. "It hurt her, you see. When my baby reached thirteen, her papa moved with her back to the States. I thought I would die of a broken heart, but I knew he was doing what he must. Soon after, I married. Sadly, I never had any children. Oh, I had a good life in Mexico. But I never forgot my baby, Laura, the child of my heart. No matter that I didn't give birth to her. She is an angel from God!"

"But Laura told us about having a mother and sisters," Biggie said.

"Yes. Her papa remarried a very fine lady who had three girls of her own. It was a blessing. Now my little one had a real family!"

"So how did you two get back together?" Biggie drained her cocoa cup and set it on the table.

Josefina took our mugs and set them in the sink. "We never lost touch, you see. Letters all the time, and once after college she came to see me in Monterrey. I came to her when she decided to open this place. My baby hasn't changed a bit. She still believes she can save the world."

"What do you think about Grace Higgins?" Biggie asked.

"That one? *Manflora!* She is not of our sort. I cry that my baby trusts her so."

"Well." Biggie stood up. "It's time for bed."

I had the room next door to Biggie, and Monica was next to me with a connecting bathroom. I rapped on her door.

"Where've you been?" she asked, opening the door.

"In the kitchen talking to Josefina."

"Well, you should have been with me. I went to find Misty, and we rode horses."

"In the dark?"

"No, silly." She flopped down on the bed. She was wearing an old tee shirt and big fuzzy slippers. "We rode in the ring. It's lighted. Boy, that Misty can jump! She's promised to teach me someday."

"Yeah, well, I gotta go to bed."

"Okay." She crawled under the covers. "Turn the light out, will you?"

I decided to take a hot bath before bed. I locked the door on Monica's side of the bathroom and started running the tub while I undressed. I was just about to step in when I heard a rap on the bathroom door.

"J.R.," Monica hissed, "come here, quick!"

"I'm undressed," I said.

"Well, get your clothes on. This is good. Hurry!"

I put my clothes back on, unlocked the door, and slipped into her room.

"Shhh." She put her finger to her mouth. "Listen!" She was sitting on the floor with her ear to the wall. "They're having a big fight."

I joined her. "Who is it?" I hissed.

"It's Babe and her husband. Now shut up and listen."

". . . always were a slut," I heard. It was Rob Parish.

"Yeah, well being married to a wimp like you would drive any woman to it. You're not a man, you're a goddamn calculator. You've got numbers where your heart ought to be."

"It's called brains, bitch. Something you wouldn't know anything about."

Monica put her hands over her mouth to suppress the giggles.

"I don't need brains, Einstein, I've got looks—and personality."

We heard a crash, like a glass breaking.

"Stop it! Let go, you're hurting me."

"Then sit down and listen. I don't give a damn if you chase after Hamp Caldwell all day long, but I promise you one thing, sister. You are not going to cut me out of my share of the old man's money. And speaking of that, we've got bigger problems than your overblown libido."

"What's that?" Monica whispered.

"Shhh! Listen!"

"Yeah, what?"

"Number one, the way that spacey stepmother of yours is spending the money, that's what. She's going to spend every damn dime on this idiotic fat farm. Number two, in case you hadn't noticed, your papa's now found himself a long-lost grandson. I heard him talking to Polk this afternoon."

"About what?"

"About changing his will, that's what."

"What can we do?"

"Here's the plan. . . ."

Now that they weren't shouting at each other anymore, their voices grew fainter. Monica ran to the bathroom and came back with a glass. She held it against the wall and pressed her ear to it. She shook her head. "Doesn't help," she said. "You want to try?"

I took the glass and listened, but it was no use. They must have moved away from the wall.

"What do you think it means?" I said.

"I think it means you need to tell Miss Biggie about this first thing in the morning. J.R., you could be in danger!"

10

I declare," Mrs. Muckleroy said at breakfast. "I can't wait to get home. I want to change into fresh clothes. I feel like a hobo wearing the same clothes I wore yesterday."

I looked at her dress, which must have cost a bunch.

"Oh, I don't mind that, but I do want to get back to town and see what damage the tornado's done." Miss Julia speared a slice of ham off the platter as Biggie passed it to her. "Umm, this looks like real ham, not that stuff you get in the grocery store nowadays."

"Where is the family?" Mrs. Muckleroy asked.

Abner spoke from the head of the table. "They're all late sleepers. I'd be happy to take you ladies—and young people—for a tour of the ranch before you leave."

"That would be great," Biggie said. "Rosebud, are the roads cleared?"

Rosebud nodded. "Got it on the radio this morning. We can leave anytime you're ready."

"Excellent." Biggie drained her coffee cup. "Then we'd best have our tour, if you can go now, Abner."

"I'll pass," Mrs. Muckleroy said. "I think I'll just relax on the patio with my second cup of coffee."

"I'll join you, Ruby," said Miss Julia.

"Then, we're off." Abner scraped his chair back from the table.

Monica and I followed Biggie and the foreman out the door.

"Have you told her yet?" Monica whispered.

"Haven't had a chance."

"The ranch is near four thousand acres." Abner swept his arm in a circle around him. "But nearly half has gone back to woods. We're clearing and planting around seventy-five acres a year. Rex is not much interested; but the way I see it, the way the money's going out around here, the quicker I can make this into a profitable operation, the better."

"I hear ranchers are going broke all over the place," Biggie said.

"That's right. You have to have a gimmick: Mine is in exotics."

"Exotics?"

"Yeah, cattle. See that bull over there. He's a Limosin. French. We sell his semen to breeders."

"My, he's huge."

"Right. I've got four more on order. We also cross-breed him with our registered polled Herefords. The calves make mighty fine beef cattle. Now over here we have our horse barn." We followed him in.

"Beautiful horses," Biggie said. "What are they?"

"Arabians. We breed those, too. Hamp and his daughter train them for sale. Ah, here comes Ol' Hamp now with his pretty little daughter."

Abner introduced Hamp and Misty to Biggie.

"I used to ride all the time as a girl." Biggie stroked the soft nose of one of the horses.

"How about a ride this morning?" Hamp lounged against a stall.

"I'm not dressed for it," Biggie said. She looked like she wished she were.

"No problem." Hamp led us into the tack room and opened a closet. "We've got plenty of riding clothes. How about these? You're about Babe's size, I'll bet." He held up a pair of riding britches.

"Well . . ."

"I want to ride, too," Monica said.

"That settles it then. J.R.?"

I wasn't about to make a fool of myself. I'd seen those dinky little saddles.

"I'll just watch," I said.

Misty and I stood at the rail as Hamp and Abner led the horses carrying Biggie and Monica into the ring.

"Your grandmother seats a horse like she was born to ride," Misty said.

"I guess," I said, surprised.

Misty giggled. "Can't say the same for your friend, though." Monica was all over that saddle as the horse trotted around the ring.

We watched as Biggie reined her horse to a stop and

spoke briefly to Hamp, who nodded his head. I like to have swallowed my tongue when I saw what happened next. Hamp and Abner pulled a barricade into the pen and set it up across the riding path.

"She's going to jump," Misty said.

I wanted to cover my eyes but didn't want Misty to think I was a sissy. Biggie turned her horse and trotted to the end of the ring. She nudged him with her heels. The horse sped toward the barricade. My heart pounded as my grandmother lowered herself across the horse's neck and sailed over the barrier. Monica, straddling her horse on the sidelines, stared openmouthed while Biggie went around again.

Later, after the ride was over, Monica couldn't stop talking about it. "Miss Biggie, that was the awesomist thing I ever saw. Where'd you learn to do that?"

"On the farm where you live—when I was a girl." Biggie smiled at Monica.

"You reckon I could learn?"

"Maybe," Biggie said. "Maybe I'll get you and J.R. a horse and teach you myself."

Suddenly, we heard the pounding of hooves as Laura rode past us. She was a good distance away and never saw us. "My, oh my, she sits a horse well," Biggie said.

"Sure does. She's a natural." Abner looked admiringly at Laura as she galloped away.

"Do you think she's good for Rex?" Biggie asked.

"Yes'm, I do. She'll do just about anything to make him happy—anything but give up this camp, that is."

"And does that make Rex unhappy?"

"No, I don't think so. Of course, he's past caring about all the money being spent. That's left for the rest of us to worry about. All in all, though, she's a good kid. She's got some mighty peculiar ideas though."

"Such as?"

"Such as all this New Agey stuff she's gone off her head about. Bunch of bull, if you was to ask me, which nobody does, of course."

Just then, Hamp whistled from the barn. He waved his arms at Abner. "Phone call!" he shouted.

"Be back pronto," Abner said, and hobbled off toward the barn. Biggie took a seat on a concrete bench, and we joined her and watched as Hamp strolled toward us.

Monica sighed. "That is one good-looking man," she said. "Even if he is old."

Hamp leaned against the fence and looked down at Biggie. "Abner'll be out in a minute," he said. "Meantime, I've got a proposition for you, Miss Biggie."

Biggie cocked her head at him.

"Well, ma'am, you're a damn fine rider. I guess you know that."

Biggie nodded. She's never been one for modesty.

"I was wondering if you'd be willing to come out once a week and give the girls lessons. Misty and I have been doing it, but we're not in your class—not even close."

"You're gonna teach them to jump?" Monica wasn't sure about that.

"Eventually. Right now, we're just teaching them to sit a horse, trot, canter—that sort of thing. The main thing

Grace wants them to do is care for the horses, but Laura says they should have some fun if they're going to have to do all the work."

"I agree," Biggie said. "Besides, it's good exercise. About my coming, I'm not sure. I'll have to think about it."

"Well, do that." Hamp turned to go. "We, Laura and I, we'd sure be happy if you could though."

"Does Laura know you've asked me?" Biggie wanted to know.

"Not yet." He smiled. "But I can assure you, she'll be delighted with the idea."

Biggie stood up. "We'd better get back to town."

As we approached the house, we saw the camp girls. Each one had a large trash bag and was picking up limbs and twigs blown down by the storm. Grace sat on a bench watching.

"Good morning," she called out when she saw us. "You're out bright and early."

Biggie looked at her watch. "Not so early," she said, looking toward the girls.

Grace saw the look. "You probably think it's wrong for us to make the girls work like this. Right?"

"Well . . ." Biggie said.

"It's part of the program, you see. Being productive brings with it a feeling of self-esteem that no amount of meaningless exercise can do. The growth process that takes place here has nothing to do with diet, really, although we do abide by certain nutritional protocols. What we offer them is a mind-body-spirit cleansing that is designed to last a lifetime."

102

Monica made a face.

"Hmmm . . . ," Biggie said.

"If I had more time, I could make you understand." Grace's face hardened. "But I'm sure you need to be on your way."

"Yes, we do . . ."

Just then Rob Parish power-walked by. Monica nudged me. He stopped briefly in front of Grace, walking in place. "I see you're still playing Simon Legree."

Grace ignored him and he marched on, elbows flapping at his sides.

11

Well," Biggie said, after we had driven about a mile toward town, "it must not have been much of a storm, only a few limbs blown down."

"Shoot, I've seen lots worse." Monica was bouncing around like a monkey trying to see out all the windows at once. "Last year a storm blew the roof off Elvis Moton's barn. It landed in a chinaberry tree a half mile away."

"Would you sit still!"

Monica didn't hear me. She was leaning across the front seat between Biggie and Rosebud. "I bet you've seen lots of storms down in south Louisiana, Rosebud."

"Hurricanes, mostly," Rosebud said. "I recollect the time Audrey come through Cameron Parish. Now that was a doozy. Dern near wiped out the town of Cameron. My Uncle Buddy . . . Godamighty, look at that!" He drove the car onto the shoulder of the road and stopped.

For once, Monica couldn't think of a thing to say, just stared openmouthed at a fifty-foot-wide tunnel through the forest swept clean by the storm. It went as far as we could see into the trees on both sides of the road. Limbs and whole tree trunks lay in piles beside the road left there by the cleanup crews. Power lines had come loose from their poles and dragged on the ground. It looked like a giant bulldozer had come through and cut away everything in its path. Tall pines were snapped in two like toothpicks and leaned this way and that, while the oaks and gum trees were stripped bare.

"I'm getting out," Monica said, going for the door. "I see a dead cow."

"Don't you move!" Rosebud barked at her.

"Huh?"

"You ain't going anywhere with those wires down. You crazy, girl?"

"Oh . . . I didn't think." For the first time in her life, Monica actually seemed embarrassed.

"Rosebud, get home quickly." Biggie pointed. "That storm path leads right straight toward Job's Crossing."

The car coughed and hesitated as Rosebud gave it the gas. I doubt if that old funeral car had ever been driven as fast as we drove getting back home.

When we came to the outskirts of town, we saw the storm's path again. It had wiped out the Fresh-As-a-Daisy café. The big sign for the Big Eight Motel lay across the parking lot, and our only convenience store, the Wag 'n' Bag, was nothing but a pile of rubble.

"Well, it looks like it missed the main part of town," Biggie said, with a sigh. "I can't wait to get back home."

As Rosebud pulled the car into the driveway, I could see Willie Mae sitting on the front porch watching for us. She got up and came down the front steps. "I knew y'all was all right," she said. But I could see a tear creeping out of the corner of her eye as she grabbed me in a big hug. "Come on in the kitchen. I got cookies and coffee already set out."

"Willie Mae, how did you know when we'd be here?"

I might as well have saved my breath. Willie Mae is a voodoo lady, and she never gives away her secrets.

"I want to go to my house," Monica said, in a little bitty voice.

Biggie put her arm around her. "Honey, I know you do. Rosebud will take you in a little while. In fact, we'll all go."

Inside the front hall, I took a deep breath, drinking in the smells of Biggie's house, furniture polish and talcum powder and, best of all, chocolate chip cookies fresh from the oven. We followed Biggie into the kitchen where we sat around the table eating cookies and telling Willie Mae everything that had happened.

"And now I've got a new granddaddy," I said.

Just then, my dog, Bingo, came skidding into the room chasing Booger, who jumped up on the counter and sat licking himself. Willie Mae swatted him with a towel.

"Hey," Monica said. "I thought you were keeping Prissy Moody."

I put down my milk glass. "I forgot! Willie Mae, have you seen her?"

Willie Mae shook her head.

"I've got an idea," Monica said. "Willie Mae, why

don't you do a voodoo spell to bring her back?"

"Yeah!" I've seen Willie Mae do some amazing things in my time.

"I got a better idea," Willie Mae said. "Why don't you two go looking for her?"

"Come on." Monica headed for the back door. "I bet I find her before you do."

I didn't have much hope of finding her after two days and a bad storm to boot, but I walked around the house and down the sidewalk thinking it wouldn't hurt to ask the neighbors if they'd seen her. Monica disappeared behind Mrs. Moody's garage. I knocked on every door on our block and some on the next block over, but nobody had seen her. As I walked back home, I thought maybe I could make some signs and nail them on utility poles around town. But the minute I opened the front door, I heard a familiar sound, a shrill, annoying bark. Prissy! I hurried to the kitchen and there she was, growling at Booger around mouthfuls of Alpo. Monica was sitting at the kitchen table with a satisfied grin on her face.

"Where was she?" I didn't know whether to be relieved or ticked off.

"Under her own back steps, of course. She'd gone home. J.R., you're such a dodo. Why didn't you look there in the first place?"

I chose not to answer that.

Later, we all got back into the car and drove out to Monica's. The farm belongs to Biggie, but the Sontags, Monica and her parents, live there rent-free for taking care of the place. When we drove into the rutty driveway, Mr. and Mrs. Sontag came running out of the house.

Monica jumped out of the car and ran toward them.

"Did y'all see that storm?" she babbled. "We did. Boy, was it a doozy. Blew away half the town. I'm not kidding."

Monica has a tendency to exaggerate.

Mr. Sontag pointed toward the barn. Its roof was gone. The chicken house was nowhere to be seen. The corral fences were broken in several places. And Buster, Monica's dog, came limping out from under the house.

"Buster!" Monica knelt to pet him. "What happened?" She looked up at Mrs. Sontag.

Mrs. Sontag, who is round and rosy like an apple, smiled. "He's just bunged up a little, honey. Daddy found him under a piece of tin that blew off the henhouse. He'll be okay in a day or two."

After Biggie wrote out a check to have the buildings replaced, we got back in the car and headed for town. Personally, I don't remember ever being so glad to get rid of Monica. She was really getting on my nerves.

After supper, Butch and Miss Mattie dropped by to find out how things had gone at the ranch.

"What kind of diet do they have those girls on?" Miss Mattie wanted to know. "I'm putting on a little myself. I might want to try it."

Butch eyed her. "More than a little, if you ask me. Mattie, you ought to exercise more. Me, I never gain an ounce. It's my metabolism. Mama used to always say, 'Butchy, honey, slow down once in a while; you're just wired like a fiddle string.' And I am. I can eat anything I want." He patted his flat stomach.

Miss Mattie ignored him. "So, tell us, Biggie, did you see Rex?"

"I saw him," Biggie said. "He seems to be in real poor health—but happy to meet J.R."

"I bet he was glad to see you, too," Butch said.

"That, too, of course."

"The diet," Miss Mattie prodded.

"I'm not sure," Biggie said. "They seemed to eat the same as everybody else."

"Not exactly, Biggie," I said. "Remember, they drank something before we ate." I turned to Butch. "They drank it out of coconut shells."

"Did they make a face when they drank it?" Butch sipped his tea with his pinkie raised.

"Not that I could tell," I said. "We're going back tomorrow. I'll see if I can find out what it is."

"You'll do nothing of the kind," Biggie said. "It's none of our business. Now, you scoot up to bed. I want to talk to Butch and Mattie alone."

I stayed awake until Biggie came upstairs. I went to her room and stood at the door in my pajamas. She stopped brushing her hair and looked at me. "What?" I told her what Monica and I had overheard. "Well," she said, "I'm not surprised they're upset at having you show up out of the blue. Don't worry about it. They can't do any harm. Now, scoot off to bed."

Lying in my bed, I thought about Monica, wondering why she got on my nerves so much lately. She had always been my best friend. I admired her for so many things.

She could ride and hunt and fish with the best of them, and if she ever met old Freddy Kruger face to face, she'd probably just walk up and spit in his eye. Next to Rose-bud, she was the bravest person I knew. Why then, all of a sudden, did she seem so . . . ? I couldn't put words to it. I was still trying to figure that one out when I fell asleep. You would think, under the circumstances, I would have dreamed of Monica that night. But I didn't; I dreamed about Misty Caldwell instead.

12

Rosebud parked the big, black limo in front of the ranch house at six o'clock Friday evening. Fat cows grazed in the pasture while the horses hung their heads over the corral looking for all the world like they were were saying, Welcome back. One even curled his lips and gave a friendly whinny. The sun, red and low in the sky, seemed to color the whole place a soft, peach color.

"My, isn't this peaceful," Biggie said. "Makes me miss the old days on the farm."

"Not me," I said. "I like living in town. It's too quiet out here."

Rosebud got out and came around the car to open the door for Biggie while I hopped out on the other side and ran up the gravel walk to ring the doorbell. Babe opened the door.

"Oh, it's you." She turned and walked away from us

toward the bedrooms. "The others are in the great room," she said over her shoulder.

Abner Putnam stood up as we came into the living room. Laura sat on a leather chair near the fireplace holding a glass of wine, while Grace Higgins sat in a matching chair opposite her. Jeremy Polk, a drink in his hand, stood facing Laura in front of the mantel. Laura jumped to her feet and walked over to Biggie, hands outstretched.

"I'm so glad you're here," she said. "Rex has been asking for you all day." She hooked her arm through Biggie's. "Would you see him now? I know it's rude not to offer you a drink first, but he seems so very anxious to see you."

"Of course," Biggie said. "Does he want J.R., too?"

"Yes, absolutely. He insisted on that." She lowered her voice. "I'm afraid my poor sweet baby's not feeling well. I hope you'll understand if I ask you not to stay long."

She led us down the hall and opened the door to Rex's room. He looked smaller than he had two days ago, and his face was the color of wood ashes. Pillows on both sides kept him upright in his recliner, and I wondered if he might just tumble over like one of those round-bottom dolls if you took them away. After Laura closed the door behind her, he motioned us to come closer. Biggie pulled up a straight chair and sat facing him.

"What's happened to you?" she asked.

A smile tried to pass across his face. "That's my Fiona," he said. "You never did mince words, did you?"

Biggie shook her head impatiently. "In two days'

time, honey, you've gone down quite a bit. Are you sick? Has the doctor seen you?"

He waved his big hand. "No, not that. I have days like this, dear. It comes and goes. Now listen, we haven't got much time before I have to take another dose of that dratted medicine. After that, I'll be as worthless as a canceled stamp."

I moved in closer so I could hear.

"I've changed my will to include young J.R. here. Fiona, I know you're a smart woman, so I'm counting on you not to let any of them pull a fast one. Understand?"

Biggie nodded. "Where is your will?"

He tried to turn in his chair and point toward the chest of drawers behind him, but the effort was too much. He slumped lower in his chair and shook his head. "It's in the—"

Just then someone knocked loudly on the door and Jeremy Polk came in. He nodded to us and walked across the room and stood in front of Rex. "Sorry to interrupt, friend, but I've got to get back to Dallas tonight. I just need a few minutes of your time—to finalize what we talked about earlier."

Rex looked irritated, but nodded. "Will you come back later?" His eyes pleaded with Biggie. "I'll put off the damned medicine somehow."

Biggie bent down and kissed the top of his head, and when she did, I saw a tear in her eye. "Sure we will."

When we got back to the living room it was dark outside. The deer horn chandelier over the couch cast weird shadows over the room. Babe was standing at a table against the wall that served as a bar pouring herself a big belt of whiskey while her husband, Rob, watched.

"That's my darling," he said, "a woman of lusty appetites."

Babe turned around, and if looks could kill, Rob would have been a dead man. She opened her mouth to speak, but then she glanced at me and snapped it shut.

"Where's Rosebud?" I asked.

"He went to the kitchen to have a beer with Abner," Grace Higgins said.

"I believe I'll go, too." I headed for the door.

"I want you to stay here with me." I could tell from Biggie's voice that it wasn't going to do any good to argue, so I sat beside her on the couch.

Laura spoke up. "Babe, honey, why don't you fix our guests a drink?"

"Sure. What'll you have?"

"I'll have a Big Red," I said, surprised to see that they had added two cans of my favorite soda to the other drinks on the table.

"Just a small glass of wine for me." Biggie sat down next to Laura. "What's wrong with Rex?" she asked, straight out.

Laura looked flustered. "Well, I . . . he woke up feeling poorly this morning. I thought he'd be better by now. He was so looking forward to your visit. If he's not better by morning, I'll call the doctor."

"He said something about his medicine." Biggie watched Laura over her wineglass. "What's he taking?"

"Well, he's diabetic, you know, so he has to take his insulin. Then, let me see, there's the heart medicine and

114

painkillers. They make him a little confused. . . ."

Just then the front door flew open and Stacie burst in. Her shirttail was half in and half out, her hair was sticking out all over her head, and her cheeks, red and blotchy, were tearstained.

"Why, Stacie darling." Laura half rose to her feet.

"Don't 'Stacie darling' me, you bitch." The girl's voice was hoarse and low. "I know who you are, remember?"

"Get a grip, kid." Babe weaved a little as she made her way to a chair. "Why don't you go back to the barn with the other cows?"

Stacie ignored her. "I've had it." Her voice rose. "I'm not staying here, and you can't make me."

"But, darling, where would you go?" Laura's voice was low.

"Stacie, stop it!" Grace rose to her feet and approached Stacie. "Stay out of this, Laura. I can handle it."

But she couldn't. Stacie made a horrible face as she grabbed Laura by the arm. Then I saw something shiny in her hand. It was a gun, and it was pointed at Laura's temple. For an instant everyone was too surprised to move.

Then Laura began speaking softly to Stacie. She spoke in a singsong voice. I couldn't make out the words, but it sounded a little like baby talk. After what seemed like a long time, Stacie's eyes softened and the hand holding the gun dropped to her side. Laura kept chanting while Grace slowly began edging her way toward them. Just as she got near enough to reach out and grab the gun, Stacie snapped out of it.

"No!" she shouted; and dragging Laura, she ran to a

115

door, pulled it open, and disappeared into the next room, taking Laura with her. We heard the lock click into place.

"What is that room?" Biggie asked.

"Laura's study," Grace gasped. "We've got to get in there."

But before she had time to move, a shot rang out, then another, then a few moments later one more. Somebody screamed from behind the door.

It must have been five seconds before anybody moved. Biggie was the first to react. "Someone phone 911," she said. "I'll go find the men."

Just then the lights went out and the room turned black as a well digger's pocket. I sat there stunned until the tiniest bit of light entered the room. I could barely make out Biggie's figure against the window. Feeling my way across the room, I came and stood next to her. She had opened the drapes, letting in a little moonlight. We both watched as something moved out on the patio; then the lights came back on, and Abner Putnam entered followed by Rosebud.

"Nothing to be alarmed about," Abner said. "But I'd like to get my hands on the SOB who tripped the breaker switch. Most likely one of those gals playing a stunt. Hey, what's the matter with everybody?"

Grace pointed toward the closed door. "It's Stacie. She's locked herself in with Laura. Hurry! She's got a gun."

In unison, Abner and Rosebud approached the door. Abner knocked and called out, "Open up, Stacie. Now, I mean it!"

Silence.

"We've got to break it down," Rosebud said.

Abner nodded and together they prepared to ram the door with their shoulders. But at that moment, the door opened and Laura stood there holding the gun. Behind her, we could see Stacie crumpled on the floor.

"Oh, my God! Is she shot?" Grace tried to push past Laura.

"No, of course not. Nobody's shot." Laura turned back and knelt beside the girl. "She's just upset. Come on, honey, stand up now."

I stood in the doorway and watched the scene. The lamp on the desk made a splash of yellow on the polished wood. The walls were lined from floor to ceiling with bookcases all holding big, dull-looking books. A huge dictionary stand stood in one corner with an open book on it. The heavy brocade curtains moved slightly from the breeze outside. Stacie began to stir.

Between them, Laura and Grace got Stacie to her feet and brought her, sobbing, to the sofa.

"Somebody get her a glass of water," Grace ordered. "And get Laura something stronger."

Babe turned toward the drinks table but stopped when Jeremy Polk came in from the hall, his hands and face covered with blood.

"Call the police. Somebody killed Rex."

13

The doctor came and pronounced Rex dead from a slug through the heart. He was tending to Jeremy, whose ear had been nicked, when the Texas Ranger, Red Upchurch, came to the door.

Biggie met him and filled him in on what had happened. They were old friends. Biggie'd helped him solve a few cases in the past, and the ranger knew he could rely on her. I guess that's why he asked her to assist him in questioning the witnesses. He told everybody to wait in the great room, and he turned the dining room into an interrogation room. I followed them in.

"Hey, what's the kid going for?" Babe seemed to be pretty drunk by now.

"Shut up, Babe." I thought for a minute that Rob was going to hit her.

Ranger Upchurch opened his briefcase and took out

a small tape recorder. He placed that on the table along with a yellow legal pad and a black pen. He pulled out a chair at the head of the table and motioned for Biggie to sit at his right. I sat in a chair against the wall, intending to be as inconspicuous as possible so they wouldn't send me away. Now the ranger went to the door.

"Mrs. Barnwell, will you come in?"

Laura sat down and crossed her hands in front of her to stop the shaking. Her face was blotchy, and her eyes red and teary. Ranger Upchurch turned on his tape recorder. After getting her to state her name and relation to the deceased, he started questioning her.

"Now then, Mrs. Barnwell, just relax and tell me what happened here tonight."

She blotted her eyes with a wadded-up tissue, then spoke in a small voice. "Well, we had planned a quiet dinner with our friends from town." She nodded toward Biggie. "Rex was eager to see them. You see, he had just found out he had a grandson he never knew he had— young J.R. here." She half-smiled at me then went on. "It seems that years ago, he and Mrs. Weatherford were . . ."

"You can skip over that part," the ranger said. "I have already taken a statement from Biggie."

"Oh, well . . ." Laura cleared her throat. "Mrs. Weatherford—Biggie—and J.R. visited with Rex for a short while. Then we all gathered in the great room for drinks before dinner. Soon after they rejoined us, Stacie came in. She's just naturally excitable, and tonight she was especially upset."

"Can you tell us what it was about?"

"Uh . . . no, I don't think I can. She's a troubled child.

Sometimes I don't think she, herself, knows what she is upset about. If you knew anything about her background, you'd understand."

"Maybe you'd better tell us a little. . . ."

"Maybe I'd better. You see, Stacie spent most of her life in the care of Child Protective Services. She was abandoned as an infant, and they never found her parents. Somehow Stacie slipped through the cracks."

"In what way?"

"Well, you see, she might have been adopted except that the agency never took legal action to have her parental rights severed, so she was shunted from one foster home to another. Some of them were pretty horrible, to hear her tell it."

"How did she end up here?" Biggie wanted to know.

Laura looked down at the table. "I found her," she said.

"And?"

"Well, that's what we do. This is not a fancy spa for rich people's children. A lot of people think it is, and I'll admit we do take in some paying guests. It helps with the bills. But mostly we try to locate needy kids who have a hard enough time making lives for themselves without also being hampered by their weight."

"All right, Mrs. Barnwell," the ranger said, "now tell us what happened here tonight."

"Well, as I said, we were having our drinks when Stacie came into the room. She was hysterical; she had a gun. When I tried to calm her, she somehow grabbed me and held the gun to my head. She dragged me into the study and locked the door."

120

"You must have been scared."

"Not really. You see, I make a point of knowing all my girls. I knew exactly how to handle Stacie. I talked to her, you know, reassured her—and, well, she handed me the gun. It was then we heard the gunshot, and the lights went out."

"Did you fire the gun?"

"Oh, no."

Biggie opened her mouth to speak, but then she snapped it shut.

The ranger clicked off the recorder. "That will be enough for now, Mrs. Barnwell. I know Mr. Barnwell's death is a terrible shock."

I looked at Biggie, but she was watching Laura leave the room. The ranger called after her. "Mrs. Barnwell, I wonder if you would mind sending in Miss Grace."

Grace told pretty much the same story. "The problem with Laura is she's too darn trusting. Most of these girls have much more going on than their weight problems. That's the beauty of our regime here. We treat the whole person: mind, body, spirit. Love and discipline, that's our theme. Laura, bless her, has oceans of love to give; but when it comes to discipline, her tank's on empty. She especially wanted to pamper Stacie, although in truth, Stacie needs a stronger hand than most. She has rebelled against the program since she came here."

"What does the program consist of?" the ranger asked.

With that, Grace launched into the whole story of the diet again. It was very boring. "I suppose you've heard of the mind/body connection?" She looked like she didn't think he had.

The ranger nodded.

"Well, first, we immerse the girls in positive affirmations. They read and study for two hours a day, only the great thinkers of our time: Norman Vincent Peale, Dale Carnegie, the Maharishi, Anthony Robbins . . ."

Biggie covered her mouth with her hand.

"That's the mind part. For the nourishment of the spirit, we use body movement, moon baths, certain yoga techniques, that sort of thing." She looked at the ranger, who nodded again.

"Now, as to the body, hard work and a sensible diet is the secret. There are no aerobics classes here, no exercise equipment. We don't believe in meaningless use of the body. Hard work, that's the answer to weight loss. When the girls see the results of a job well done, they get a real sense of accomplishment."

The ranger stood. "Thank you, Miss Higgins. You may . . . oh, one other thing. What is your impression of Laura Barnwell?"

Her face softened. "She is the sweetest, most adorable . . . no, let me restate that. She is my business partner; and with the exception of the matter of discipline, we are of one mind about the services we offer here. It is my hope that what happened tonight will not put an end to that."

After she left the room, the ranger turned to Biggie. "What do you think?"

"About what?"

"Both those women. Start with Laura." The ranger got up to make sure the door was closed, then came back and sat down.

"She means well, I think." Biggie poured a glass of water from the pitcher on the table and took a sip. "Do-gooder, of course—thinks she can save the world. Makes me think of Ollie Sistrunk. She goes to our church. Awhile back, Ollie decided chickens were getting a raw deal. She'd seen them being trucked around town about forty chickens crammed into these little bitty cages—and she'd seen some TV show about cruelty to chickens. So she organized a march out to Birdsong's Fresh-As-a-Daisy Chicken Farm and Processing Plant to protest. Naturally, she didn't get many marchers, doncha know, since a good number of folks in town work out at that plant."

The ranger nodded, then tried to get Biggie back on track. "But what do you think about Laura?"

"I'm getting to that," Biggie said. "Ollie sent out letters to the editor and posted signs all over town. She started raising chickens herself just to give them good homes. After a while, people started making fun of her and calling that big house of hers Cluckingham Palace."

"So what happened to her?" the ranger couldn't help asking.

"Her husband finally sent her off to a sanitarium. She had gone completely off her head. That's what happens sometimes when people go overboard."

"And you think Laura's done that?"

"Could be," Biggie said. "It's getting late. Who's next on your list?"

Ranger Upchurch went to the door and called in Abner Putnam. He looked even more upset than Laura had. He sat down at the table and mopped his brow with a blue bandanna.

"I understand you and Rex were pretty close," the ranger said.

"We were buddies." Abner frowned.

"So you were good friends."

"Oh, sure, the best of friends. I would have laid down my life for old Rex—and he'd have done the same for me. We'd been together for, let me see, going on thirty years now."

"Do you know anybody here who would have wanted him dead?"

Abner looked shocked. "Wanted Rex dead? Who would want that?"

"Apparently somebody did," Biggie said softly.

"Okay." The ranger picked up the tape recorder and looked at it, then set it back down. "Suppose you just tell us what you were doing this evening."

"Sure. I spent the afternoon helping Hamp vaccinate the horses. After that, I went to the bunkhouse to take a shower and change clothes. Then I came up here to the house."

"And?"

"I came in through the back door to find out what Josefina was cooking for supper. She was making tamales, so I sat at the table and helped her roll them up—you know, spread the shucks with masa dough then put in the meat and all." He looked at the ranger who nodded. "After we got 'um tied into bundles and on the stove to steam, I got me and her a beer out of the icebox, and we had just sat down when Rosebud walked in."

"What time was that?"

"Sundown. Around six-thirty, I reckon."

"And you were all still sitting there when the shots were fired?"

"Yeah, but we didn't hear the shots. The kitchen's too far away from the bedroom wing. But when the lights went out, I went right straight to the breaker box to check on it."

"Right. And where is the breaker box?"

"In a piss-poor place, if you ask me. 'Scuse me, Miss Biggie. Some fool mounted the thing on the wall outside by the patio. I checked the box and found that the switch had been intentionally turned off."

"How could you tell?" Biggie wanted to know.

"Easy. You see, if the thing trips from an overload or some such thing, the switches only move over halfway, but when somebody turns it off manually, it goes all the way over."

The ranger nodded like he understood.

Biggie opened her mouth to speak, then snapped it shut again. She stood up. "Well, it's late, and J.R. has school tomorrow."

"Then go," Ranger Upchurch said. "I'll drop by the house tomorrow to get Rosebud's statement."

14

So who do you think done it?" Willie Mae asked after we got home and were all sitting around the kitchen table eating chili and drinking cocoa.

"No idea," Biggie said. "Jeremy Polk is the logical suspect since he was with him at the time—only he was shot, too."

"Bad?" Willie Mae got up and poured more cocoa all around.

"No. The bullet just grazed his ear."

"Who all was in the living room when the lights went out?" Rosebud asked. "Seems to me none of them could of done it."

"Let me see," Biggie said. "Grace and Babe and Rob—us, of course. And Stacie had taken Laura into the study. I guess that clears all of them."

"Well, Abner and Josefina were settin' right there in

the kitchen with me." Rosebud stretched his legs out in front of him, crossing his ankles. "Reckon that clears them."

"That leaves Hamp or one of the girls," I said.

"Not necessarily," Biggie said. "It wouldn't have to be someone connected with the ranch. Anyone could have crept up to the house and shot through the window. And since the breaker box was on the outside, they could have shut the power down, too."

"Biggie," I said, "the driveway's long. If anybody drove a car up it at night, somebody would have seen the lights."

"What about the gun?" Willie Mae wanted to know.

"Don't know yet." Biggie stood up. "Red will be coming by in the morning to take a statement from Rosebud. I'm sure he'll fill us in on that. I'm going to bed. It's been a long day."

I was awake half the night throwing up. Biggie said it was probably the three bowls of chili I ate, but she let me sleep in the next morning just in case. When I finally came downstairs I felt fine, but it was already past eleven and too late to go to school. I went into the kitchen.

"Boy, was I sick last night," I said to Willie Mae.

"I ain't surprised," she said. "You want me to fix you some milk toast?"

"With an egg in it?"

Willie Mae nodded and put a pan on the stove to boil. "Go wash your face and comb your hair," she said, her back to me.

Willie Mae and Biggie are sticklers for neatness. When I got back from the bathroom, a bowl of steaming hot milk poured over buttered toast with an egg on top was waiting for me. I poked the egg with my fork and watched the yolk run out. Prissy crawled out from under Biggie's desk and came to sit by me. I held a piece of toast just out of her reach to tease her. Willie Mae frowned and poured some warm milk in Prissy's bowl for her. She was lapping it up when Mrs. Moody came in the screen door. Prissy liked to have busted a gut jumping all over her.

"There's my baby girl," Mrs. Moody said, picking Prissy up and hugging her. "Mama missed her little dumpling. Did my little snookie-ookims miss her mama?"

"How come you be back so soon?" Willie Mae asked, pouring Mrs. Moody a cup of coffee.

Mrs. Moody sat down at the table holding Prissy on her lap. "I had to," she said. "Those kids of Woodrow's about drove me crazy. They don't know the meaning of the word 'no.' Spoiled to death is what they are. Not that I'm the least bit surprised what with the mama they've got. And poor Woodrow, he works his fingers to the bone driving that bread route. He's just too tired to discipline them when he gets home."

"So who's taking care of them?" I asked.

"Oh they're all in school now. I found a teenager to come in after school and look after them 'til Woodrow gets home. I told Woodrow, I said, you just get that wife of yours back here. A woman's first responsibility is to her husband and children, is what I always say. Anyway, that old mama of hers is a whole lot better. If she'd had the sense of a goat, she never would have . . ."

I pushed my plate away. "Where's Biggie and Rose-bud?"

"Rosebud's gone to the store for me, and Miss Biggie's in the living room talking to that ranger."

"I better go see," I said, and headed for the living room as fast as I could.

Ranger Upchurch was perched on Biggie's sofa having a cup of coffee and telling Biggie all he knew about my new grandfather's murder. He had a hat line crease in his red hair, which he always has when he takes off his big Stetson.

"Anyway, that's about all we know now," he said. "I'm going back out right after lunch, and I was wondering if you'd be willing to go out and ask a few questions on your own."

"Why should those people talk to me?"

The ranger laughed. "Now, Biggie, don't pretend with me. You know they'll talk to you if you want them to. You could get information out of a dead man."

"Dead men often tell more than the living," she said.

"Biggie, that doesn't make a bit of sense," I said.

"She means evidence, son." Ranger Upchurch stood up and put his hand on my shoulder. "Things you find out without having to ask questions."

"Oh. Can I go, Biggie? I might be able to help." I was thinking I might see Misty again, but I didn't let on.

Biggie felt my forehead. "You feeling okay?"

"Yes'm."

"Then I don't see any harm in it."

When we drove up to the ranch house, Butch's van with Hickley's House of Flowers painted on the side was parked out front, and he was hanging a black wreath on the front door.

"I believe this is the prettiest one I ever made," he said.

I took a close look at the wreath. "I never saw any black flowers before."

"It's my own invention," Butch said. "Isn't it just gorgeous? What I did was, last night I set a bunch of red carnations in a coffee can full of black ink. They just drunk up that ink like it was water, and by morning it had turned them all black. I may get a patent on this. It could revolutionize the funeral business."

"Butch, you're a wonder," Biggie said. "But how did you know so soon that he was dead?"

"Biggie, you know how word travels in this town. Arthel Reid, the new undertaker, called me just as soon as he got his hands on the body. We help each other like that, doncha know. Professional courtesy."

"Anybody else around?" Rosebud asked.

"Sure. They were all sitting around the dining room table when I got here. Well, ta-ta, gotta go. The Methodists are having the bishop this Sunday, and they want to load the church up with flowers." He waved two fingers at us and headed for his truck.

Rob Parish answered the door looking as dorky as ever. His hair, black and straight, hung over his forehead, and his rumpled white dress shirt had a big ink stain on the sleeve. His too-short pants rode up enough to show the white socks he wore with a pair of black Oxfords. He frowned when he saw us but motioned us to follow him into the living room. A mess of papers covered the top of the coffee table.

"Where is everybody?" Biggie asked.

"Who knows?" he said. "All over, I guess. My darling wife is still sleeping it off, and Laura took a pill and went back to bed right after lunch. What do y'all want?"

"Just a courtesy call," Biggie said, taking a seat in one of the wing chairs by the fireplace.

Rob sat on the couch in front of the coffee table. "Well, I'm working here."

"Oh, go right ahead. Don't let us disturb you." Biggie's not easily discouraged. She sat for about five seconds before she asked, "What's that you're working on?"

He pawed through the papers, not looking at Biggie. "It's a book I'm writing."

"Oh, a book! Then you're an author! How exciting. What's it about?"

"It's a novel—a serious novel."

"My gracious, aren't you smart. Do tell me about it. I'm so interested in reading."

I hid a smile. Biggie never reads anything except the newspaper. She's too busy doing other things.

"It's about good and evil, love and hate, power and corruption."

"My, oh my," Biggie said. "Tell me more."

Rob couldn't resist. The way I saw it, probably not many people asked him to talk about his work.

"Well, there's this young man, he's a kind of Christ character. Good, you know, and pure. Well, he sells his soul to the devil for gold and power."

"How original," Biggie murmured.

"Yes, I thought so. So, anyway, he meets this rich man, and the man has a daughter. She's very beautiful but evil. The boy is bewitched by her charms, and soon they are married. The rich man gives his daughter a fortune for a dowry."

"How nice," Biggie said.

Rob frowned at her. "No, you miss the point. It was not nice at all. The young groom had planned to use the money for good, but his wife has other ideas. She spends recklessly on frivolities. The young man begs her to stop, but she only spends more, so he goes to the father for help. He tries to reason with him, earnestly pleading that the money be used for humanitarian purposes. The father laughs in the young man's face, for he is Beelzebub himself, you see. In the end the girl becomes a drunken shrew. She mocks the boy and makes his life a living hell."

"And what happens to the father?" Biggie looked sharply at Rob.

"Justice prevails." Rob picked up the papers and began sorting them in neat piles. "I haven't got it all worked out yet."

"One more question, honey," Biggie said. "This is so interesting. . . . I was just wondering, does the old man have a wife?"

Rob's face took on a goofy look. "Yes, he does. A beautiful creature, as good as she is kind. Try as they might, the old man and his evil daughter cannot corrupt her. In the end, she and the young man—"

"Well, that sounds just wonderful." Biggie stood up

and went and stood at the French door that led to the patio. "Oh, there goes Grace. Sorry to rush off, honey, but I really want to compliment her on the fine job she's doing out here with the girls."

I rolled my eyes and followed Biggie outside. "Biggie, how do you know she's doing a good job?"

"I don't, but I want to talk to her. Now, hush, here she comes."

Grace Higgins looked like a woman with a purpose when she stepped from the grass onto the brick patio. She nodded curtly when she saw Biggie heading her way, and tried to step around her, but Biggie was too quick and grabbed her in a big hug. "Honey, we just came out to offer condolences. I know you all must be so broken up about poor . . ."

Grace stood with her arms hanging at her side looking down at Biggie. "That's nice of you, but I have to—"

"See Laura, I'll bet," Biggie said. "She's taken a pill and gone to bed, so I'm afraid you'll have to wait. There doesn't seem to be anyone else around, so I thought you and I might have a little chat."

Grace thought a minute, then I guess good manners got the best of her. "Oh . . . all right. I have a minute or two."

"Good." Biggie drew two chairs up to a wrought-iron table and took a seat, leaving the other for Grace.

"Now." Biggie's tone suddenly got businesslike. "I haven't been entirely honest with you. I'm here because the ranger asked me to help him investigate poor Rex's murder. You can help a lot if you'll just answer a few questions."

Grace's mouth dropped open. "He asked *you?*"

"In the past, I've done my bit to help the authorities when murder's been done. Of course, I'm only an amateur . . ."

"Well, I don't know what I can tell you." Grace folded her hands in front of her. "You were there when the ranger questioned me last night."

"Yes, but I have a feeling that you're a bright woman and a good judge of character. Am I right?"

"I try." Grace relaxed in her chair. "Okay, ask away."

"Let's start with Rex," Biggie said. "How long have he and Laura been married?"

"Umm . . ." Grace wrinkled her brow. "About eleven years, to the best of my memory. Soon after I returned from the Peace Corps, I ran into Laura in Lansing, Michigan. Soon after, we became roommates. We both had jobs but just barely scraped by. Rex had quit racing by then and was designing futuristic prototypes for new cars. He and Laura met at a car wash, if you can believe that. Romantic, huh? But he apparently was swept off his feet by her, as who wouldn't be. And Laura? Well, what girl could help but . . . I mean he rushed her something awful. She was impressed with all that money and power." Grace gripped her hands together until her knuckles turned white. "I really, I don't think she ever really loved him, but she was dazzled. He was handsome then and drove a hot little sports car. . . ." Her voice faded and she stared at the pasture beyond the house.

"So how did you all come together here?" Biggie asked.

Grace kind of jumped like Biggie's voice had startled

134

her. "It was about two years ago. By then I had gone back to school to become a dietitian, and Laura knew it. We'd kept in touch, you see. So when she called me all excited about this project for the girls, I'll admit, it gripped my imagination, too. So, as they say, the rest is . . ."

". . . history, I know," Biggie said. "So what are your thoughts on Babe and Rob?"

"Leeches, the two of them. Babe has been bad news all her life as far as I can tell. Her mother divorced Rex when Babe was very young, and the kid never had much to do with her daddy until she heard he'd married Laura. Then out of the blue she showed up, all lovey-dovey and wanting to be part of his life. Rex, of course, was flattered and welcomed her with open arms. As for Rob—well, you've met him. Enough said?"

Biggie nodded. "Well, thanks for your time. Are there any plans yet for a funeral?"

"Yes. As soon as they release the body, he'll be buried here on the ranch. Graveside services only. Rex wasn't much for religion, and those were his wishes." She got to her feet. "Now, I really do need to talk to Laura."

"Sure, honey. Run along now. You've been a big help."

We watched as Grace disappeared through the French doors, then Biggie jumped up. "Come on," she said. "Let's find the ranger. I want to have a word with him."

15

We found Ranger Upchurch talking to Hamp out by the horse barn. Misty, looking cute as a basket of kittens, in jeans and cowboy boots, was saddling a horse. I went over to talk to her.

"Goin' for a ride?" My mouth was full of cotton, and I couldn't think of another thing to say.

She smiled at me. "Uh-huh. Want to come along? I can saddle Blade for you. He's real gentle."

I looked at that saddle. "I, um . . . I don't know. I may have to be getting back to town."

She must have read my mind. "I could put a western saddle on him."

"I'll see," I said, and headed back to where Biggie was standing beside the ranger.

"Go," she said when I asked her. "Just be back in an hour."

We walked the horses past the corral and the riding ring and across the pasture until we came to a grove of trees.

"Watch your head and legs," Misty said. "Old Blade will try to knock you off. He'll either cut too close to a fence post, or sometimes he'll head for a low limb and try to scrape you off that way."

"I thought you said he was gentle," I said.

Misty laughed. "You always have to be smarter than the horse. They're just like people; they have their little quirks."

I ducked as we passed under an oak tree and followed Misty through the woods into a wide clearing bordered on both sides by planted pines.

"This is a pipeline right-of-way," she said. "They keep it mowed, so it's a perfect place to run the horses. Come on!"

She nudged her horse with her heels and cantered away. I gave Blade a nudge, but all he did was speed up to a trot, all the time trying to get his head down to the green grass below. Finally, I gave him a good kick and held on to the saddle horn as he galloped after Misty. We must have ridden a half mile when we came in sight of a blacktop road up ahead. Misty reined in her horse and waited for Blade to catch up.

"This is the end of the trail," she said. "I know a good place to rest and let the horses drink. Follow me."

We turned the horses left and entered an even denser wood than before. Grapevines trailed from the trees and ran along the ground, causing the horses to step high to avoid them. I could hear gurgling water, and soon we broke into a clearing beside a creek bank. Misty jumped from her horse and led it to the water. I followed suit. After the horses had a drink, we tied them to a low-hanging branch and sat down on the mossy ground.

"I didn't know you rode," Misty said, smiling.

"Oh, sure." I didn't tell her that the only riding I'd ever done, except for the ponies at the county fair, was on Mr. Sontag's old mule.

"You should come out and ride often." She leaned back on her hands and looked sideways at me. "That is, if we're staying here, me and Daddy, I mean."

I sat up straight. "Why shouldn't you?"

"I heard them talking, Abner and Daddy. Abner was saying they might have to sell the ranch. He said Rex had already settled a bunch of cash on Laura, and he wasn't leaving her anything in his will."

"That's awful." I watched two beetles crawling across the green moss pushing a ball of dung. "What will y'all do?"

"Daddy'll move on to another job, I guess. He's a wonderful trainer. Before we came here, he trained quarter horses, you know, for racing. That's big business, and good trainers get paid a lot. Actually, what Daddy really wants to do is settle down with his own stables, but you have to have lots of money for that."

"Where's your mom?"

"She's married again and living in Arizona. I've got a little brother there, but I've never even seen him. When she and Daddy divorced, she gave me to Daddy. I guess she didn't want me." Misty didn't look sad, just matter of fact.

"Cool—I didn't mean that. It's not cool when your mom doesn't want you around. What I meant to say is, my mom didn't want me either. I guess we have something in common. Does it bother you her not wanting you?"

"Uh-uh." Misty waved away a gnat that was buzzing around her face. "I'd lots rather live with Dad."

"Me, too—I mean, I'd rather live here in Job's Crossing with Biggie."

Misty turned and put her face close to mine. "J.R., I've never met a boy as nice as you. Have you ever heard of soul mates?"

"Huh?" I was having a hard time breathing.

"Soul mates. People who were meant to be together. I was reading this book one time . . ."

"Would you like to go to the junior high homecoming dance with me?" I knew my face was turning red, but I forced myself to look straight at her. "It's next Friday night, and Rosebud could drive me out to pick you up. We'd bring you home, too."

Misty's face lit up with a big smile. "Sure! You are just the sweetest boy to ask me." With that, she gave me a kiss right on the lips. I hate to admit it, but I was so surprised I fell over backward and rolled down the hill, just barely stopping myself before I fell into the creek. When I looked up, Misty was laughing her head off. I laughed, too, because what else could I do?

Back at the horse barn, I said good-bye to Misty and went to find Biggie. I found her sitting at a picnic table under some trees talking with Rosebud and the ranger.

139

"He had a gun," Ranger Upchurch was saying.

"He always kept it in his bureau drawer. Anybody could have gotten their hands on it."

"And in the shape poor Rex was in, he'd never have known." Biggie's lips drew into a thin line.

"The funny thing is," the ranger said, "the gun the kid had—it had been fired. Rex's gun, we're not too sure about."

"Did anybody find a slug?" Rosebud asked. "In the study, I mean."

Ranger Upchurch shook his head. "Not a sign. And Mrs. Barnwell says Stacie never fired the gun."

Biggie opened the car door and got in. Then holding the door open, she said, "Red, I'm worried about the daughter, Babe."

"I am, too," the ranger said. "I plan to have a talk with her before I leave here today. The funeral, such as it is, is tomorrow. Will you be coming out?"

"I haven't been invited," Biggie said. "Still, I believe it's my Christian duty to comfort the grieved, so I might just bring along a casserole for the family."

"That's my girl." The ranger grinned and slammed the door. He stood watching as Rosebud turned the car around and drove away.

That night at dinner, I told my news. "Misty's going to the dance with me. I asked her, and she said yes. Rosebud, I told her you'd drive me out to pick her up." I spooned gravy on my mashed potatoes. "I might need to borrow some money to buy her a mum. I want Butch to make a big, fancy one with lots of streamers hanging

140

down—and little doodads attached to the streamers, just like the high school girls have. Will you loan me the money, Biggie? I'll rake leaves or chop wood—" Suddenly, I noticed everybody had stopped eating. "What? What's the matter?"

Biggie had been cutting her chicken-fried steak. "J.R., you've already asked Monica to the dance."

I had forgotten. Two weeks ago, Monica and I had gone fishing at Wooten's Creek. I had caught a big catfish. For once Monica had bragged on me a lot, telling me not just anybody could have landed him, that it took a real fisherman to do that. Later, we had fired up Mr. Sontag's outdoor fryer, and we'd cooked my fish and eaten him for supper. After supper, we sat out on Monica's back steps and tried to pick out the constellations in the summer sky. Just when I was getting ready to leave, full of catfish and pride, I had asked Monica to go to the dance with me.

"Well." I thought fast. "I don't . . . I don't really think Monica's into that kind of thing. She goes to that little country school . . . she wouldn't know anybody . . . and besides, she probably doesn't even have a dress to wear." I took a sip of tea. "She'd more than likely be embarrassed when nobody asked her to dance. Isn't that right, Rosebud?" I looked at Rosebud, but he was cutting his meat. "I guess I'll just call her and tell her . . ." What would I tell her? Suddenly, I wasn't hungry anymore. "May I be excused?"

Biggie nodded. Nobody said a word as I got up from the table and went up the stairs to my room.

16

The next morning when I came down for breakfast, Willie Mae was making my favorite breakfast, French toast made from thick slices of homemade bread with lots of cinnamon and powdered sugar sprinkled on top. A pitcher of warm maple syrup sat on the table.

"Hurry up and eat," she said, "you gonna be late for school."

"I don't feel like going today." I pulled the syrup pitcher toward me. "I think I've taken a virus."

"The love bug done bit you," Rosebud said, coming in from the back porch. He sat down at the table. "When that old love bug bites, he causes a feller to do stupid things."

"Rosebud, I don't . . ."

Just then the telephone rang. Biggie, dressed in her

turquoise jogging suit, came down the backstairs and picked it up. "Hello. Um-hum . . . How did you find out? Well, Julia, I don't know about that, all of us going . . . Oh, you're going anyway? . . . Well, okay. We'll pick you up at four. . . . You're taking baked beans? I don't know yet. I have to talk to Willie Mae about it. All right. You be ready now, you hear? Okay, bye."

"What was that all about?" Willie Mae wanted to know.

Biggie went to the stove and poured herself a cup of black Louisiana coffee, then sat down at the table. "Oh, it's Julia and them. Julia's found out the funeral is this afternoon, and she insists that we all go out and take food to the family. Says it's our duty as good Christians."

"Well, Biggie, you said the same thing. . . ."

"Don't be a smart mouth." Biggie poured syrup on her French toast. "I intended to go by myself. They'll just be in the way. Oh well, it's done. Rosebud, can you drive us out at four?"

Rosebud nodded. "I got to get the oil changed first."

"Biggie, I don't feel like going to school today."

Biggie felt my forehead. "There's not a thing wrong with you."

"Well, don't you need me to go to the ranch with you? You always say I'm a big help. . . ."

"J.R., we're not going until four. Just get yourself home right after the bell rings."

The trunk of the limousine was filled with casseroles and fried chicken and potato salad when we finally drove out of town. Biggie's club, the Daughters, which she's president of, had organized a food committee. Miss Julia and Mrs. Muckleroy had been appointed to go along and serve.

"Stop by the shop and pick up Butch," Mrs. Muckleroy said when we picked her up. "He wants to ride out with us."

"Why didn't we just put a notice in the paper and invite the whole town?" Biggie grumbled.

"Why, Biggie, we couldn't do that!" Miss Julia was shocked. "Half the riff-raff in the county would invite themselves along. Ooh, there's Butch. Stop here, Rosebud."

Rosebud pulled the car up to the curb in front of Hickley's House of Flowers and Butch, wearing black velvet jeans and his white ruffly shirt got in. He held a covered cake plate.

"Did you bake a cake?" Miss Julia asked.

"Not likely," Butch replied. "I got one of Populus's cherry pies. They're my favorite. Which kind do you like, Ruby?"

"Coconut," Mrs. Muckleroy said. "I just naturally gravitate toward the cream pies, myself."

Mr. Populus is Greek and owns the Owl Café, which is downtown on the square. It's called the Owl on account of a long time ago, it stayed open all night. Now, Mr. Populus closes at nine, but the people in Job's Crossing were used to the old name, so he never changed it. Mr. Populus makes the best pies in the whole world—even better than Willie Mae's, although I'd never want her to hear me saying that.

Biggie rode in front with Rosebud while the other grown-ups lined up in the back. I had taken the small jump seat.

"Ooh, I've just got chill bumps running up and down my spine." Butch wriggled around in his seat. "Girls! Has it occurred to you that we're headed right straight into danger? A killer's on the loose at that ranch."

"You do what you must," Mrs. Muckleroy said. "Myself, I just put on the armor of the Lord." She held the cross she was wearing up so everybody could see.

"That's right, we all have to make sacrifices." Butch examined his fingernails. "Darn! I've chipped my polish."

"Well, y'all can call yourself Christian soldiers all you want to," Miss Julia said. "Me, I'm just filled up with curiosity. What's going on out there, Biggie? Do they know who the killer is?"

"Not yet," Biggie said. "Red Upchurch has sent both guns off to be tested."

"Both guns? You mean there were two? Mercy, that must have been quite a night," Mrs. Muckleroy said.

"It was, for a fact," Biggie said. Then she told about Stacie coming in and taking Laura hostage. "Of course, her gun wasn't the one used to kill Rex. That was his own gun."

"Then why send the other one off at all?" Miss Julia asked.

"Just because it was there, I guess," Biggie said. "It was right there in the room next to us the whole time. But Red is very thorough. He doesn't leave anything to chance."

"I'm that way, too," Mrs. Muckleroy said. "Oh, here we are. Where are all the cars? I thought they had a funeral out here."

"Family only," Biggie said. "Park over here by the fence, Rosebud."

The ladies went in the front door while Rosebud and I took the food around back to the kitchen. Josefina, dressed in black, was standing by the stove stirring a pot. When she looked at us, her eyes were red from crying. Then when she saw what we had, I thought she was going to start bawling all over again.

"What is this?"

"The ladies and Butch brought y'all some food," Rosebud said. "Where you want it?"

"Why?" Josefina asked. "Can't I cook for this family?"

"It's a custom," I said. "Whenever a person dies, folks take food. Where do you want it."

"Over there, I guess." She motioned toward a table that stood against the wall.

Rosebud sat down at the kitchen table to talk to Josefina, and I went looking for Biggie. I found her sitting alone with Babe in the dining room. Babe was wiping her eyes with a tissue.

"He was the only living soul who loved me just the way I am," she said. "What am I going to do without him?"

"Where is your mother?" Biggie asked.

"Dead. She and Daddy divorced when I was seven. I went with Mama. She kept me until she couldn't anymore."

"Couldn't? Surely Rex took care of the two of you. Financially, I mean."

"Oh, sure. Mama had breast cancer. We lived in Wisconsin where Mama had a good job with the state. She never married again. She always said, after Rex Barnwell, no other man would do."

"Then why did she divorce him?"

"Oh, she didn't. *He* divorced her. Of course, I was just a kid at the time. But from what I could piece together later, Daddy was gone a lot and Mama had, you know, men friends . . ."

"I understand," Biggie said quickly. "So how old were you when your mom got sick?"

"A teenager, about fifteen, I guess. She worked as long as she could, even when the chemotherapy made all her hair fall out. Finally, we had to go and live with her sister in her small house in Madison. That's when Mama sent me to live with my daddy." She pulled a fresh tissue out of the box and blew her nose. "It was just fine at first. . . ."

"Then Laura came along?"

Babe looked at Biggie. "Laura? No, Laura had nothing to do with it. We got along okay until I married Rob. That's when the trouble began."

"Do you want to talk about it?"

Suddenly Babe's face hardened. "No, I don't think I do. Why are you asking so many questions anyway? Are you a cop or something?"

Biggie patted her hand. "No, honey, just an old friend of your daddy's."

"Well, I have to find Hamp. He's promised to take me riding. Lord knows, I need to get away from this house. It's giving me the creeps."

With that, Babe got up and hurried out of the room.

"What do you know about that?" Biggie said. "Well, come on. I want to pay my respects to the Widow Barnwell."

I followed Biggie through the great room where the ladies and Butch had Rob cornered and were asking questions a mile a minute. We went down the hall to Laura's room where Biggie rapped on the door.

"Who's there?" It was Laura's voice.

"Honey, it's Biggie Weatherford and J.R. Can we come in?"

The door opened and Laura stood there. She was wearing a long, floaty robe, pale blue. I could see a matching satin nightie under it, and she had on tiny slippers to match. Her brown hair was loose and fell in waves around her face. She looked as pretty as a field of bluebonnets.

"Come in," she said, real soft. "I'm sorry, I can't talk very well. All the crying has done something to my voice, I think."

"Saltwater," Biggie said. "Best thing in the world. Just gargle a little—warm—every thirty minutes. You'll be good as new."

"Thanks, I will. Come in, please. I was in bed. Do you mind if I just climb back in?"

"Of course not, honey." Biggie pulled a blue velvet chair from the dressing table and placed it next to Laura.

I stood at the foot of the bed. "Are you all right?" Biggie asked.

"Not really." She sniffed like a little girl. Biggie handed her a tissue from the box on the bedside table. "To tell the truth, Mrs. Weatherford, I don't know what I'll do without Rex. Oh, not that I don't think he's in a better place now. The poor man suffered so this past year. I'm selfish, I guess. But, you see, even as sick as he was, Rex was my strength. Can you understand that?"

"Of course," Biggie said. "He's always been that way, even as a boy."

Laura smiled at Biggie. "I forgot, you knew him, too. I guess we share something . . . I don't know how to say it . . ."

"You don't have to," Biggie said. "Now, what's to happen to you—to the ranch?"

"Oh, well, the girls need this place. Somehow, we have to carry on."

Biggie nodded. "What about Babe?"

"Babe?" Laura looked surprised. "Why should you ask about her? She'll go on with her life, I guess. She doesn't live here, you know, although she and Rob stay here a good part of the time. They have a house in Arkansas—up in the hills. Rob thinks of himself as a writer, although I don't think he's ever published anything. I can't see why they would continue to come here. Babe scarcely hides her dislike for me."

"And you? How do you feel about her?" Biggie looked hard at Laura.

Laura sighed. "I tried to be her friend at first, really.

But Babe didn't want that, not for a minute. I can't prove it, but I have a feeling she tried to undermine me with her father. When she was still in high school, she used to spy on me. She didn't think I knew it, but I did. Even if I was only going to the grocery store, she'd follow me in her car." She stared out the window at the ivy trailing down from the house. "Once I confronted her about it when I caught her lurking outside the beauty salon, but only once. She became hysterical and accused me of things you can't even imagine. After that, I left it alone."

"Did you tell Rex?"

"Actually, no. Babe would have accused me of trying to cause a rift between her and her father—and, who knows, Rex might have believed it. We hadn't been married so very long when all this was happening."

"It sounds to me like that girl needed professional help."

"Oh, we sent her to counseling—the best money could buy. But she fooled the therapists. They would call us in for family sessions, and Babe would be all sweet reason. Eventually, I think, they ended up thinking we were terrible parents."

"My, my," Biggie said. "I guess you won't be sorry to see her go then?"

"Sadly, no. It was clear long ago that Babe and I could never be close, even now when we share the same sad loss." She closed her eyes and put her head back on the pillow.

Biggie stood up. "Honey, all this talk's just wearing you out. We'll be going now." She patted Laura's hand

and headed for the door then turned back. "By the way, I was just wondering . . . do you know when the will's going to be read?"

Laura didn't answer. Her eyes were closed, and she looked to be asleep. But she wasn't asleep; she was playing possum. I could see her eyelids fluttering.

"Are we going home now?" I asked Biggie.

"In a minute," she said. "I just want to check Rex's room one more time."

I followed her down the hall and watched as she pushed open the door, noticing that someone had taken down the yellow crime tape. The room was dark and smelled nasty.

"What is that smell?" I whispered.

"It's death, J.R. You can't wash away the smell of blood. It lingers for a long time." She switched on the lights and began to walk around the room, picking up things and setting them down, opening drawers and pawing through the contents. I looked at the pictures and trophies on the mantel. My grandfather had been a great man, I could tell. In one picture, he was standing with Paul Newman beside a sleek, white racing car. In another, he was talking to Larry King. I wondered what was going to happen to all these things now.

Finally Biggie touched my arm. "Let's go," she whispered.

I followed her to the door. Just as she was reaching for the knob, she bent down and examined the wide baseboard next to the door. "There's something lodged here," she said. "And it looks to me like a bullet. See if you can find me a tool to dig it out."

"I don't have to, Biggie. I've got my pocketknife with me." I dug the knife out of my pocket, half expecting to get into trouble for carrying it, but Biggie didn't say a word, just took it and went to work on the slug.

17

By the time we got home, the wind had turned to the north and the temperature had dropped twenty degrees. Willie Mae had made beef stew with plenty of tender meat, potatoes, peas, and baby carrots swimming in rich, brown gravy. She set a plate of hot cornbread on the table to go with it. For dessert, we had crispy fried peach pies. When we finished eating, Willie Mae poured coffee and set cups in front of Biggie and Rosebud. She sat back down at the table.

"You find out anything today?" she asked Biggie.

Biggie sipped her coffee and frowned. "I'm not sure. I certainly found out something about the goings on in that family."

"They don't like each other much," I said.

"That's right," Biggie said. "The only thing they all seemed to agree on was that they loved Rex."

"And he be the one got hisself kilt," Willie Mae commented.

"That's right," Biggie said. "And I'm too tired and full of your good supper to think about it anymore." She got up and stretched her arms above her head. "Rosebud, I think we could have a fire in the fireplace tonight. What do you think?"

"Suits me," he said. "I just cleaned the flue last week. She's all ready to go soon's me and my boy here bring some wood in."

"Rosebud," I said, as we loaded the wood onto the wood cart, "I'm in big trouble."

"You sho is."

"How do you know what I'm talking about?"

"It's plain as mouse turds in a sugar bowl." He grinned at me, showing the little gold hearts, clubs, diamonds, and spades he had built into his front teeth.

"Rosebud!"

He leaned against the woodpile and crossed his arms. "Anybody who gots two women on the string's got trouble. Um-hmm."

"Well, what am I going to do about it?"

"Help me get this wood in the house, and I'll be thinkin' on it."

Once we got the wood loaded in the big copper pot Biggie uses for a wood box and Rosebud had a fire going in the fireplace, I prodded him. "Did you think of anything?"

"What?" Biggie had been dozing in her chair.

"Rosebud's supposed to be helping me with a problem I've got."

"I ain't what you'd say necessarily *supposed* to do nothing. Still and all, it does put me in mind of the time a black feller I knew got hisself in a similar jam."

"What am I going to do, Rosebud?"

"What do you want to do?"

"That's just what I don't know. Monica's been my best friend ever since . . . forever. But Misty, she's different from any girl I've ever known. I feel like I've *got* to take her to the dance. It's not like I've got a choice, Rosebud, I gotta do it!"

"I see what you mean. But, make no mistake about it, boy, you *got* a choice!"

I sighed. "Well, what happened to the feller?"

"It happened when he was working on a cattle ranch down in south Texas."

"I never heard of a black cowboy."

"They's lots of things you ain't heard of. Now, shut up and let me tell this story. You see this feller needed to make some money so he could marry up with his sweetie back home in Natchitoches where he come from. Naturally, it didn't take him long to figure out there wasn't never any money in wrangling, but that's another story. Anyhow, they put him up in a bunkhouse with a bunch of Mexican vaqueros who didn't speak one word of English."

"They spoke Spanish."

"Ain't you smart? Of course they spoke Spanish, and fast, too. Wellsir, this feller got awfully lonesome, listening to the others rattling away in a language he couldn't understand. Finally, after a while, he began to pick up a word or two here and there, enough to get by on the job, but not much more. Even the foreman spoke Spanish. He used to lay in his bunk at night while they played some card game he couldn't make head nor tail of thinking of his sweetie back home. She wasn't much to look at, a little-bitty thing with a face like a raisin. And sometimes she'd talk to that feller like he had a tail, but boy could she cook." Rosebud laughed without making a sound and slapped his knees. "She could put together a fine gumbo that would make you stand up and slap your grandpa. And sweet tater pies? Umm-umm. Still and all, there was something else about her, something more important than her cooking, something he couldn't rightly put his finger on. He thought it might be the way she didn't seem to care what anybody thought about her, the way she'd say and do whatever she took a notion to, exactly like as if she had a sprig of mistletoe hanging from her coattails, if you take my meaning. It was like that she knew a secret that nobody else in the whole world knew. It made this gal awfully attractive in a way that this feller never really understood.

"Anyway, one weekend he went into town and wandered into a honky-tonk on the back street. You can't imagine how pleased he was when he discovered a musician playing blues music on an old piano. Well, he thought he was back home again. He ordered himself a beer and pulled his mouth organ out of his pocket, and when that piano player launched into 'Saint James Infirmary,' he commenced playing along. When the song was over, everybody in the place whooped and yelled and bought him beers. The pretty little gal behind the bar gave him a big kiss on the mouth."

"What's a mouth organ?"

"A harmonica. After that, every chance he got, he'd go in that bar where they liked him and spoke his language. He'd play his mouth organ until closing time, and everybody, especially the gal behind the bar, treated him like he was somebody special. Pretty soon he began to believe it. He forgot why he'd come to the ranch in the first place."

"Why was that?"

"Pay attention, son. He was supposed to be saving up his money so he could marry his little sweetie back home."

"Oh. So what happened?"

"He took to waiting until the gal, Rosa, got off from the bar at night so he could walk her home. Some nights he wouldn't get back to the bunkhouse until the sky was turning gray in the east. Needless to say, he didn't get much sleep on account of they had to get up at the crack of dawn to do their work. Well, one day they was ropin' calves—"

"Do they really do that? Outside of rodeos, I mean."

"Shoot yeah, they do. They had to get 'um in the pen to vaccinate them. Well, this feller, he was so groggy from not getting any sleep that he somehow got both arms tangled up in his lasso and, before he could stop it, he'd done broke both his wrists. Well, naturally, they fired him."

"That's cold."

"It ain't cold. A wrangler with two broke wrists ain't no more good than tits on a boar hog. Besides, it was his own fault he done it. But the feller didn't see it that way.

157

He just felt sorry for himself. So soon's the doctor put splints on his wrists, he headed into town to get a little sympathy from Rosa."

"I feel kinda sorry for him."

"So did he. Well, he walked into the bar and first thing, everybody started clapping and calling for him to get out his mouth organ. He didn't do nothin' but put on a pitiful face and hold up his bandaged wrists. He sat down at the bar and ordered a beer with a straw and waited for somebody to ask what happened to him."

"And did they?"

"Nope. Not even Rosa. She spent the whole night talking to a feed salesman from Corpus. Well, he went back to the bunkhouse and got his gear and headed down to the bus station to take the next bus back to Natchitoches."

"So he married his sweetie back home?"

"Yeah, he married her—but it taken him ten long years to do it."

"How come?"

"On account of he'd done messed with her; and a gal like that, she don't take kindly to bein' messed with. But he always said, she was worth the wait."

"And I guess the sweetie is Monica and Rosa's Misty and I'm your friend."

"I never said he was my friend, did I?"

"I guess not."

"He wasn't my friend because he was me. And that little sweetie down in Natchitoches was Willie Mae. I was lucky; you might not be."

"Rosebud, I'm only thirteen."

Rosebud stood up and brushed the wood chips off his pants. "I know that. But you got a chance to learn something important here. Think about it. Looks ain't important; character is."

I stood up. "I know what you're getting at, Rosebud. Monica's Willie Mae and Misty's Rosa. Well, it just isn't so. Monica's just an old country girl, and Misty would never be mean. She thinks we're soul mates. She told me so! I'm going to bed!"

As I climbed the stairs, I heard Biggie laugh and say something to Rosebud. I went into my room and slammed the door.

The next day was Saturday, and I woke up feeling pretty good considering the dilemma I'd gotten myself into. Booger was curled up in a ball at my feet, and my dog, Bingo, lay beside him. That was unusual because as a rule Booger does not care for Bingo at all. I pushed them down and got dressed in a hurry. I was thinking I might call up DeWayne Boggs, and the two of us could ride down to the bypass to inspect the tornado damage. We might find some good stuff among all that rubble.

When I got down to the kitchen, Biggie and Rosebud were sitting at the table eating eggs with grits, ham, and red-eye gravy. I went to the fridge and poured myself a glass of orange juice and joined them just as Willie Mae set a full plate in front of my chair.

"Yum," I said.

"You look right pert this morning." Rosebud pushed his plate away and took a sip of coffee. "For a man with gal trouble, that is." He winked at Biggie.

"I'm gonna call up DeWayne and see if he wants to go bike riding." I changed the subject.

159

"Better wear your jacket," Biggie said. "It's nippy out there."

"Yes'm. Is there any muscadine jelly?"

"I gotta open some." Willie Mae took a fresh jar out of the pantry and twisted off the lid. She used a knife to remove the layer of white paraffin from the top and set the jar with a spoon in front of me. I dug into the jelly and spooned some onto my toast.

Willie Mae poured herself a mug of coffee and joined us at the table. "What you goin' to do today?" she asked Biggie.

"I need to work on the Daughters' account books. Essie Moody was treasurer this past year, and you wouldn't believe the—"

Just then the phone rang. Biggie went to her little desk and answered. "Hello . . . yes. Well, if you think we need to be there, of course. . . . Ten o'clock? That's awfully soon. Oh, well, we'll get there as fast as we can."

"What?" I asked, pretty sure my plans were about to change.

"That was Jeremy Polk calling from the ranch. He went to Dallas to get Rex's will from his safe. Now he's back, and he wants us out there for the reading. We have to hurry."

I scooted upstairs to comb my hair and splash on some of the men's cologne I'd gotten for Christmas last year. When I got back downstairs, Rosebud wrinkled his nose and rolled his eyes, but didn't say anything.

I relaxed in the backseat of the limo feeling mighty pleased that I was about to see Misty again. If I'd known what was in store for us that day, I would have felt a whole lot different.

18

We arrived at the ranch house a few minutes before ten. Jeremy, still wearing a bandage over his left ear, met us at the door.

"Come into the dining room," he said. "The others are already gathered there."

We followed him into the room where he took a seat at the head of the table. Laura sat at his right, dressed in riding clothes. Grace Higgins was hunched next to her, leaning close and whispering in her ear. Babe sat on Jeremy's left. Her eyes were red from crying, but that didn't keep her from scowling at everyone who came into her sight. I didn't see her husband, Rob, anywhere. The others at the table were Abner, looking uncomfortable, and Josefina, looking even more out of place. As we were being seated, Hamp came in with Misty at his side.

Jeremy, who had been shuffling the papers in front of

him, looked up at the group and began to speak. "Rex wanted to do everything he could to divide his estate in a fair manner," he said. "I'm not sure you all will agree that he succeeded." He picked up a sheaf of papers stapled together with a blue cover. "Now, let me see, 'I James Carroll Barnwell, being of sound mind,' blah . . . blah . . . blah." His eyes rode down the page. He looked up. "Just getting to the meat of the thing. Umm, okay, here's where the bequests start."

"My God, Jeremy. Didn't you write the thing? You ought to know it by heart." Babe squirmed in her seat.

"Umm, yes, well . . ." He began reading. "'To my only daughter, Frances Faye Barnwell, I leave her grandmother's diamond ring.'"

Jeremy took a small, velvet box out of his pocket and slid it across the table toward Babe. "He asked me to give you this. You do understand that your father intended the large sum of money he transferred to you recently to constitute your portion of the estate?"

Babe nodded and opened the ring box. She took out a diamond ring big enough to choke an elephant.

"Why, that's worth a fortune!" Laura said, softly.

"You are so right," Babe said. "And he left it to me." She got up and left the room.

"Ahem," Jeremy said. "Moving on . . ." He ran his finger down the page. "'To my beloved wife, Laura, I leave my ranch, including all buildings and improvements to same, comprising two hundred ten acres out of the James Royce Wooten Survey, Kemp County, Texas.'"

"What?" Grace almost screamed. "He didn't leave her any *money?*"

Jeremy looked at her. "If I may continue?" He resumed reading. "'In addition, I leave my wife all my stock in the Ford Motor Company.'" He turned to Laura. "That is a small fortune, Laura. If you're careful, you should be just fine."

Laura nodded, but Grace glowered.

"Now," Jeremy went on, "'to Jason Caldwell, otherwise known as Hamp Caldwell, who has been like a son to me, I leave the sum of one hundred thousand dollars. And to my best friend, Abner Putnam, I leave the mineral and royalty interests in and to the above-mentioned two hundred ten acres in Kemp County, Texas. And there is one last bequest. To Josefina Garza, I leave the sum of ten thousand dollars.'" He folded the will and stuck it in his briefcase.

Grace sighed. "Well, I guess that means we can continue with our work here."

Jeremy held up his hand. "There's more. The day before he died, Rex made a codicil to his will." He reached into his briefcase and pulled out a handwritten piece of paper. He read it aloud to us. "'To my grandson, James Royce Weatherford Jr., I leave the sum of five hundred thousand dollars to be held in trust for him until he reaches the age of twenty-five years. I name as trustee of said monies, his grandmother, Fiona Wooten Weatherford.'"

"Wow!" I breathed.

"There's more," Jeremy said. "'Further, I leave to my said grandson, certain of my personal belongings, to wit, all trophies, souvenirs, photographs, and other memorabilia related to my career in automobile racing and design.'"

I looked at Biggie. She smiled and squeezed my hand.

Nobody said much after that as they pushed back their chairs and moved toward the door. Only Josefina raised her voice. "Lunch will be served *uno momento*. I will bring it into the great room."

I was disappointed to see Hamp and Misty leave by the French doors. Laura slipped out the door and headed down the hall toward her room, and Grace left, saying she had to see to her girls. I followed Biggie and the others to the great room.

After a lunch of *chalupas*, which, in case you don't know, are crispy fried corn tortillas piled high with refried beans, spicy meat, chopped lettuce and tomatoes, guacamole, sour cream, and grated cheese, I wandered outside, leaving the adults sitting around sipping iced tea and discussing the will.

I found Misty perched on the rail fence watching the fat girls riding in the horse ring. They were all dressed in riding britches with white blouses. They had black helmets on their heads. Grace was standing in the middle, barking orders.

"Stacie, keep that back straight. . . . Melanie, you're forgetting to post!" I saw Stacie shoot Grace the bird when she wasn't looking. I looked at Misty, who had seen it too, and was grinning.

She cocked her head at me. "I hear you're going to be rich."

"What? Oh, you mean the will. I guess so—someday. Biggie says I can't spend any of the money until I'm grown unless she decides to let me." I made a face. "That'll be the day. Biggie's tighter than the bark on a hickory nut tree. She says if we invest the money, I'll have a small fortune by the time I go off to college. I reckon your daddy's gonna be rich, too."

"Oh, I don't know. A hundred thousand is not so much. Daddy says he may be able to buy a nice piece of land with it though. Maybe start up a vet business. He doesn't think Laura and Grace will be able to keep us on here."

My heart sank. "Does that mean you'll be moving away?"

She put her hand on my arm and looked straight into my eyes. "I hope not, J.R. Not after we've just met."

I felt the heat running up my neck and turning my face red. "Would you really be sorry?"

"Of course I would. Uh-oh, Grace is letting the girls ride outside the ring." She pointed to where Grace had lowered the rail and was guiding the girls on their horses toward the road we had taken to the clearing.

Suddenly I heard the pounding of hooves and Laura came streaking by on a black horse, her hair loose and flowing behind her. Her face was as white as a sheet, and she was clinging to the horse's neck while the reins, which had slipped from her hand, hung free.

"Oh, look, she's on Midnight. He's wild! Daddy!" Misty scrambled down from the fence and raced toward the barn. I sat frozen. The scene seemed to be taking place in slow motion, as the black horse galloped straight toward a dry creek that cut through the pasture.

Biggie and the others came running down the hill toward us. I watched as Abner grabbed a lasso from the fence and pounded off in the direction the horse had

165

taken with Rosebud panting behind. The horse slowed at the dry creek, giving Abner a chance to raise the lasso and send it spiraling toward the horse's head. It hesitated over his head then fell short, barely grazing the horse's ears before it dropped to the ground. We all watched helplessly as the horse jumped the creek and raced toward the woods. Rosebud and Abner headed back to the barn.

Grace had fainted dead away and lay on the ground, surrounded by the girls who had scrambled off their horses where she fell and were all crying and talking a mile a minute. All but one, who sat on her horse like a stone, watching.

Babe watched the men going toward the barn. "What are those fools doing? She's getting away!"

"Going to saddle horses," Biggie said. "They'll never catch her on foot."

Suddenly I heard an earsplitting scream, and someone yelled, "Mother!" Then Stacie turned her horse's head, gave him a kick, and galloped off in the direction Laura had taken. Just as it came to the edge of the woods, Laura's horse reared, and she tumbled to the ground. Stacie slid off her horse and fell on top of Laura, howling like an animal.

Biggie turned to Babe. "Go up to the house and call 911. Hurry!" Then she started across the rutty field toward Laura and Stacie. Rosebud and Abner, now mounted on horses, reached them first and pulled Stacie to her feet. Laura lay, still as death, with a gash across her forehead that bled a red river down her bone white face. Her legs stuck out at an angle that could only mean both were broken. Stacie sank to the ground and sat cross-legged, like a tear-stained Buddha, still making that ungodly sound.

19

You should've been there, Willie Mae, she was broken up awful bad. I wouldn't be a bit surprised if she isn't dead by now. Blood was running down all over from a big old cut on her head, and she was skint up like you wouldn't believe."

Willie Mae set a pan of potatoes and a knife next to me. "Peel these while you talk," she said.

I picked up the knife and commenced peeling the potatoes. "Where you want me to put the peelings?"

"Get you a sack out of the pantry. Where'd the ambulance take her?"

"To the hospital, of course." I went and grabbed a grocery sack out of the pile in the pantry and set it on the floor at my feet to catch the potato peels. "Willie Mae, you ought to know that."

"Don't be smart. I mean did they take her here or over to Tyler?"

"Here, I guess. Biggie and Rosebud are there now."

"No, I ain't," Rosebud said, coming in the back door. "Miss Biggie sent me home and said she'd call when she's ready for me to fetch her. Is this coffee fresh?"

Willie Mae nodded, and he poured himself a cup and sat down at the table.

"How's the lady doin'?" Willie Mae asked.

"Not well," Rosebud said. "She won't wake up. And she's got a whole bunch of broken bones. They're afraid to try to set them on account of the anesthetic, doncha know, her bein' in a coma and all. Then that there Grace Higgins is going around getting in everybody's way and telling the doctors what to do."

"Well, I don't see why Biggie has to stay," I grumbled.

"Sounds to me like they needs somebody what gots some sense out there." Willie Mae peered into the refrigerator. "I need some butter to go in these potatoes."

"I'll go," I said, shoving the pot full of potatoes toward Rosebud, "if Rosebud will finish peeling."

"You all heart," Rosebud said, picking up the knife and plucking a potato out of the pot.

I jumped on my bike and headed downtown to the Piggly Wiggly, where I picked up a pound of butter for Willie Mae. On the way back, I happened to pass the Owl Café. Sitting inside at the big round table in the middle of the room was Butch, eating a big piece of apple pie and talking with Miss Julia, Norman Thripp, and Mr. Populus, who owns the café. The pie looked awfully good, so I decided to join them.

"Hey, J.R.," Butch said, talking around a mouthful of pie.

"Hey," I said, taking a seat at the table. "What kind of pie you got today?" I asked Mr. Populus.

"Chocolate, cherry, lemon, opple, and peenopple," Mr. Populus said. Being Greek, Mr. Populus doesn't speak English too well.

"I'll have chocolate," I said, "and a Big Red."

Butch and Miss Julia looked at each other and made faces.

"What?" I asked.

"Just doesn't sound very good," Butch said. "What's Biggie up to?"

"She's at the hospital." I watched as Mr. Populus set my pie and drink in front of me, then I took a bite.

Norman Thripp, who is as long and thin as a mashed snake, looked at me with his ball-bearing eyes. "How come she's at the hospital? She sick?"

"Uh-uh." I took a swig of my Big Red and remembered to wipe my chin with my napkin.

"Oh, Lordy," Butch said. "Has something happened to Rosebud—or Willie Mae?"

"Uh-uh. Biggie's out there seeing about Miz Laura Barnwell, who fell off a horse and is pretty near dead. It happened right after they read my granddaddy's will, which said I'm going to get five hundred thousand dollars." I took another bite of pie.

"My soul." Miss Julia took her little notebook out of her handbag. "Tell me the facts, J.R."

I told her everything I could remember, not leaving

out the part about Stacie acting like a crazy person. "I wouldn't be surprised if she wasn't in the hospital, too. More than likely wrapped up in a strait jacket."

"And he didn't leave his own daughter any money?" Norman Thripp said. "That don't seem right."

"Well, he did leave her a big, huge diamond ring," I said.

"I'd sure like to see that," Butch said.

Just then the front door darkened, and Rosebud strode in. He pointed to me.

"Oops," I picked up my sack of butter. "I got to go." I dropped some money on the table and followed Rosebud outside to the sidewalk.

"You better get to the house fast," he said. "Miss Biggie's done home, and Willie Mae's ready for her butter."

When I got to the house, the table was set in the dining room. I went straight to the kitchen and saw that Willie Mae had made chicken fried steak, mashed potatoes, butterbeans, and hot biscuits.

"How come we're not eating in here?" I asked, handing Willie Mae the butter.

"Miss Biggie's invited that Ranger Upchurch for supper," she said. "You go get washed up."

I went up the stairs and found Biggie sitting at her dressing table combing her hair. I plopped down on her bed and waited for her to say something.

"Where have you been?" she asked.

"Downtown," I said. "Willie Mae sent me on an errand. How's Laura? Is she dead?"

"No, she's not dead—not yet anyway. She's in bad shape, J.R."

171

"What about Stacie? I was tellin' 'um down at the café. I said I bet they had her tied up in a strait jacket by now. That girl's not right, Biggie."

"I agree." Biggie opened a bottle of hand lotion and poured a little in her palm. "Only she's not in the hospital"—she rubbed her hands together—"she's run away." Just then the doorbell rang. Biggie stood up. "That must be Red. Go get washed up as fast as you can. Supper's about ready."

Boy, can that ranger eat. I ate two big slabs of chicken fried steak with mashed potatoes, gravy, and two biscuits. But he ate three and then piled on another helping of potatoes and beans for good measure.

"My, oh my, I like to see a man with an appetite," Biggie said, passing around the biscuits. "But don't forget to save room for pie. We'll have that in the parlor with our coffee."

Biggie had roses in her cheeks, and I noticed she'd powdered her nose and put on a little pink lipstick.

For some reason I was already full of pie, so I sat and watched Booger and Bingo while the others had their dessert. Bingo was taking a nap in front of the gas logs. He wouldn't have been sleeping so good if he'd known Booger was stalking him. Booger walked into the room, sniffed Bingo's tail, and went and crouched under the coffee table shaking his behind. The cat sprang. Bingo yelped as Booger's claws sank into his ears; and before you could blink, he took off after Booger, who streaked out of the room with his ears back.

Biggie shook her head. "J.R., go put those two outside."

I caught both animals and shoved them out the back door. When I got back the ranger had opened a file and he and Biggie were looking at the papers in it. "So, Biggie, as you can see by the ballistics report, the bullet that killed Rex and the one that grazed Jeremy Polk came from the gun Stacie had, not Rex's gun."

"How?" I asked. "I mean that gun never left the study."

"That's right." Biggie looked at the papers. "Laura had it in her hand. We all saw."

"And they never left the room," I said. "We were all outside the study door."

"What about fingerprints?" Biggie asked.

"Just what you'd expect," Ranger Upchurch said. "Stacie's and Laura's only. Rex's gun had his prints along with Abner's. Abner says he cleaned the gun for Rex just last week."

Biggie took a sip of coffee. "Did your people dust the breaker switch for prints?"

"Naturally." The ranger took another sheet of paper from the pile. "They lifted only one good print, and it was Abner Putnam's. Of course that switch is just big enough for one finger at a time. When he turned it back on, he could have obliterated any prints that might have been on there before."

Biggie nodded. "So what do you think, Red?"

"I think it's too damn bad Mrs. Barnwell is out of commission. She has some explaining to do. In the meantime, I've got to question the girl, Stacie. She may be the only one who can give us any answers—ever."

"Is Laura gonna die?" I asked.

173

"Maybe," Biggie said. "She's in bad shape. The doctor says her brain is swelling. If they can't stop it, she will either die or be left with brain damage. That could happen even if they do stop the swelling." She looked at the ranger. "So how many bullets were fired from the gun Stacie had?"

"Three. We dug one slug from the bookcase in the study. One was lodged in Rex's body, and the third . . ."

"The one you found, Biggie," I said.

"Right. That had to be the bullet that grazed Jeremy Polk."

"What's next?" Biggie asked.

"I was hoping you had an idea." The ranger frowned.

"I'd like to go back out tomorrow and have another look," Biggie said. "Want to come along?"

"Can't." He drained his coffee cup and watched while Biggie refilled it from the china pot on the table. "I have to be in court in Center Point. I'd sure appreciate it if you would take another look—maybe ask a few more questions. Somebody might be sitting on information they don't even know is important. Oops, excuse me." He pulled his pager from his pocket and examined the little screen. "Mind if I use your phone, Biggie?"

Biggie nodded. "Use the one in the hall."

We waited quietly until he came back, Biggie examining the papers on the coffee table and me staring at the blue-and-orange flames darting up from the fake logs in the fireplace. When the ranger came back, he had his hat in his hand.

"I need to get out to the Barnwell ranch. Abner Putnam wants to organize a search party to find Stacie."

"Good idea," Biggie said, following him to the door.

174

20

As soon as breakfast was over the next morning, Biggie went into her room and closed the door. I went to the phone to call DeWayne Boggs, hoping that now would be a good time to ride bikes down to the bypass to look over the storm damage. Before I was finished dialing the number, Rosebud put his big hand on my shoulder.

"Don't be makin' no plans, boy," he said. "We got yard work to do."

"Rosebud! I was planning to go look over the tornado damage."

"You ain't got no business messin' around that stuff. We got our own damage right here at home." With that, he turned me around and marched me out the front door. Sure enough, although I hadn't noticed before, the yard was a jumble of limbs and twigs that had fallen during the storm.

"Here," Rosebud said, handing me a rake. "You rake while I use the chain saw on these here big limbs."

I was stuffing a plastic trash bag full of stuff I had raked together when I thought of something. "Rosebud, how would it be if I got DeWayne or somebody to take Monica to the dance?"

"Reckon you could," he said, not looking at me.

"What's wrong? I know what you're thinking. You don't like that idea, do you?"

"Since when can you read minds?"

"You know what I mean, Rosebud. I'm asking your advice here."

Rosebud stopped raking and grinned at me. "Okay, I was thinkin' about that time Monica knocked him down and sent him home cryin' to his momma. What makes you think DeWayne wants to go to no dance with her?"

"Oh, yeah. I forgot. That was the time DeWayne called her 'Cue Ball.' I guess I'll have to come up with another plan. It's a cinch nobody else is going to agree to take her. I only thought of DeWayne because he's so nerdy, he'll never get another girl to go out with him."

Rosebud picked up a bag and started around the side of the house. "Here comes Miss Biggie. You see what she wants while I tote this stuff out to the alley."

"Get cleaned up," Biggie said, panting a little from running. "We're going out to the ranch."

Later, on the drive out, she filled us in. "They haven't found Stacie yet," she said. "Abner has the neighbors out combing the woods."

"What if she isn't in the woods?" I asked. "What if

she got on the highway and got a ride? She could be far, far away by now, Biggie."

"The Department of Public Safety has been notified. They've put out a statewide alert for her. Anyway, I want you and Rosebud to help the men while I take another look around the house."

As it turned out, the search party had already left, so I helped Biggie in the house while Rosebud and Josefina made coffee and sandwiches for the searchers. We started in the little study. Biggie went through the desk drawers, even though the sheriff's men had already searched. She took everything out of each drawer, looked it over, then replaced it. After she was through, she took all the books off the bookshelf and shook them before putting them back. I stood at the French door looking out at the rolling pastures. The horse that Laura had been riding was grazing with the others just as if he hadn't, only yesterday, almost killed a woman. I turned the handle and pushed at the door, but it was locked. I twisted the deadbolt knob and pushed again, but the door still wouldn't open. Then I noticed that the ground outside the door was planted with chrysanthemums, gold and bronze and purple all mixed together.

"Biggie, this is funny. This is a door, but somebody has planted flowers right in front of it and it won't open."

"So? Maybe they just chose not to use that door."

"There's something else, Biggie. Looky here. These flowers are brand new. See how the dirt is all loose around them?"

Biggie squatted down so she could get a better look.

"You're right. Let's go outside and check this out."

I followed her into the dining room where she pushed open the French doors and trotted down to the path toward the study. "My soul," she said. "These plants *are* new. Look, they still have the nursery tags on them." She dug around the base of one plant. "J.R., they're still in the plastic pots. Someone must have been in a real hurry to set them out."

I squatted back on my heels and looked at the locked door. "Biggie, I remember something—about the night of the murder."

Biggie stood up and brushed the dirt off her hands. "What's that?"

"Well, when I first looked into this room—you know, right after we got the door open—I noticed that the drapes were drawn shut."

"That's right, I remember," Biggie said. "So what?"

"They were blowing in, Biggie. Those windows, or doors—whatever they are—were open that night. Why do you suppose they're locked now? Somebody must have planted these flowers to make it look like they were never used."

"I think you're right. Good work, J.R." She turned and went back into the house through the dining room doors. I followed her back into the study, where she continued to look through the books.

I watched her. "Biggie," I said, "you must have an idea. You always do."

"Well, I don't this time." She put the last book back on its shelf. "I'm through in here. Hmm, what next? I know, let's investigate Laura's room."

I followed her as she marched down the hall and stopped in front of the door. "Did she say we could look in her room, Biggie?"

"Nope." Biggie was already rummaging through Laura's closet. "But I'm sure she would if she could talk. Help me get this box down, honey. There's a stool you can stand on."

I climbed up on the stool and took down a hatbox from the closet shelf. Biggie took it from me and placed it on the bed. I watched as she lifted the lid and began to take things out, stacks of letters held together with rubber bands and photos still in the developers' envelopes. In the bottom, we found paper clips, used pencils, ballpoint pens, rubber bands, outdated postage stamps, and other odds and ends. It looked like someone had emptied a desk drawer in there. I picked up a tiny plastic bracelet, the kind they put on patients in the hospital, only this one would have just about fit Booger's paw. The words, BABY JANE DOE, were printed on it.

I held it up. "What's this, Biggie?"

She took it and held it under the bedside lamp. "Looks like a hospital bracelet for a newborn. The ranger should have this." She slipped it in her pocket and opened an envelope full of snapshots. Parking herself on the edge of the bed, she flipped through them. "Nice," she said. "Rex and Laura on a ski vacation." She handed one to me. "He was nice looking, wasn't he?"

"I guess."

She looked at the pictures for a long time before selecting one of Rex alone. He was standing at the top of a mountain, surrounded by bright blue sky, and looking like he was just about to ski down. His face was tanned, and he was laughing. "The ranger doesn't need this," Biggie said, slipping that photo into her pocket with the baby bracelet. She started putting things back into the box. "Put this on the shelf and then we'll see if the searchers have come back."

We found Josefina and Rosebud in the kitchen. Trays of sandwiches lay on the scrubbed pine table. Rosebud was opening bags of chips, while Josefina stirred a pot of soup on the stove.

"How can I help?" Biggie asked.

Josefina put her to work setting out napkins, glasses, and soup bowls. I slipped out the back door and headed for the barn. The girls were sitting around the picnic tables under the trees chattering to each other and drinking sodas. I figured Grace must be at the hospital with Laura. Otherwise, those girls would have been working out—or just working. I waved and pushed open the corral gate. Misty stood in the barn lot grooming one of the horses.

"You like horses better than people, don't you?" I asked, just to make conversation.

She looked at me seriously. "Horses are better than people."

"Really? You think so?"

She put down the brush she had been using and started toward the barn. "Let's have a cold drink."

When we were seated in the tack room with our drinks, she said, "I never had much chance to make friends with other kids. Daddy and I, we've moved around a lot. I've met a lot of snooty kids, but a horse is, you know, just the same to everybody. They don't tell lies or suck up to you just because you've got money or nice clothes and stuff." She looked down at her canned drink.

Personally, I think horses are just dumb, but I wasn't going to tell her that. "Are you going to the dance with me?"

"We'll see," she said. "Hey, J.R., I've got an idea. How would you like to go out and find Stacie?"

"Huh?"

"I think I know where she might be hiding. See, there's this cave out there. I found it once when I was riding alone, tracked a possum in there. The opening is hidden by a bunch of grapevines. Those guys will never find it."

"How come you think Stacie knows about it?"

"Because, the day I found it, I came back and told Abner. He said it was an old Indian cave. Stacie was being punished for not making up her bed exactly right and Grace was making her muck out all the stalls. I'm pretty sure she heard us talking."

"And you didn't tell the searchers that?"

"I forgot, J.R. I just this minute thought about it."

I looked up at the house. "How far is it?"

"Not far. Come on, let's saddle the horses."

"I should go and tell Biggie . . ."

She looked at me. "You have to tell her everything you do?"

"No!" I said. "No, I don't. Let's go."

We took the same route we'd taken the first time, only now we crossed the clearing and entered the woods on the opposite side. These woods were dense. The trees, mostly gum, oak, and dogwood, dripped grapevine and

181

smilax that swagged from their branches like garlands on a Christmas tree. I called out for Misty to wait.

"If I lose you, I'll never find my way out of here."

"That's okay," she said. "We're here." She jumped off her horse and tied the reins to a low-hanging branch, leaving enough slack for the horse to graze in the soft green grass. I did the same and followed her toward what looked to me like a solid wall of green. She squeezed past the vines with me following close behind.

Inside it was dark and smelled like mud. I heard water running somewhere. Behind us, a curtain of green branches provided the only light in the place.

"Did you bring a light?" I asked.

"Didn't think about it." She took my arm. "It's scary, isn't it? Will you protect me if a bear comes out?"

I thought about Monica. She would never have said a thing like that. In fact, there have been times when she's had to protect me. Still, it felt good to be asked. "Sure," I said, hoping my voice sounded braver than I felt. "What shall we do now?"

"I don't know. What do you think?"

"Let's call her: Stacie! STACIE! Are you in here?" I put my two fingers in my mouth and whistled the way Rosebud had taught me.

Then we waited.

"Stacie!" Misty called. But it wasn't very loud.

"Shh," I said. "I think I hear something." It was a low moan. I sure hoped it wasn't a bear—or, more likely, a cougar. "Stacie?" I called again.

"Here." The voice came from the back of the cave. We both hurried toward the sound, sliding a little on the slippery cave floor.

"Where are you, Stacie?" I asked. "Say something."

"Over here." Her voice was barely audible.

I walked bent over with my hands stretched out in front of me. Finally they touched something soft and damp. "Is that you?" I whispered.

"Ouch. Yeah, it's me. Go away and let me die."

"How come you want to die?" I asked. "We went to a lot of trouble to find you. And a lot of other people are looking for you, too. What's the matter with you?" I was getting irritated.

"Come on, Stace," Misty said. "You don't really want to die out here, do you?"

"*She's* dead," she said with a sob. "I don't want to live without her."

"That sounds pretty dramatic," I said. "Now come on, let's get you out of here."

"No!" she kicked her feet toward us.

"Stacie," Misty said, "did you think Laura was killed in the accident? Is that why you ran away? She's not dead. She's in the hospital in Job's Crossing and probably worried sick about you. Now get up and come on out of here."

"Not dead? Uh-uh. You're just telling me that. I saw her, and she was dead." But there was a little glimmer of hope in her voice. "Really? She's not dead?"

"Not only is she not dead," I said, "but you're a hero for saving her life. Now, get up from there and come on!"

Stacie was filthy and sore from spending the night in that damp cave, but somehow we managed to get her on top of my horse. I rode home behind Misty with my arms around her waist.

183

21

When we got back to the house, we found the others sitting around the big dining room table eating. Grace, who had just returned home from the hospital, was giving a report on Laura's condition. Her face looked splotchy, like she had been crying, but now she spoke in a strong voice.

"The doctor says the next few hours will tell the tale," she said. "If she wakes up, it's possible there won't be any brain damage. If she remains in a coma—well, nobody knows."

"Why'd you come home anyway?" Abner barked. "Somebody ought to be there with her."

Grace gave him a dirty look. "Don't you think I wanted to stay, you old fool? They sent me home. Said I could only come back after I'd had something to eat and a little rest. Speaking of which . . ." She pushed her chair back from the table. It was then that she noticed us standing at the door, Stacie looking a lot like a cow that had been stuck in the mud.

Biggie reached us first. She put her hand on Stacie's shoulder and looked into her eyes. "She seems to be in shock," she said. "Rosebud, get her on the sofa. Somebody bring blankets. Quick!"

"Should we call the doctor?" Grace asked, her voice trembling.

"No!" Stacie said.

"Let's wait and see," Biggie said. "She may just need rest and food. Are you hungry, honey?"

When Stacie nodded vigorously, Josefina headed for the kitchen and came back carrying a mug of soup. She sat down beside Stacie and began spooning it into her. Stacie made little grunting sounds as she slurped down the soup. She rolled her eyes at Grace.

"It's okay," Grace said. "All diets are suspended for now."

"Now," Biggie said, standing up and facing Grace. "You go get some rest. Later, after this young lady has had time to recover, she has some explaining to do." She looked down at Stacie, who nodded as if she knew exactly what Biggie was talking about.

"Fine." Biggie walked over to a table against the wall and picked up her big black purse. "Come, Rosebud and J.R. We'll just go home for now." She turned to face Abner. "We'll be back at seven with Ranger Upchurch. I expect we're on the verge of having this whole matter cleared up."

*   *   *

Later, at home, I asked Biggie what she meant by that, but she wouldn't tell me a thing, just said I'd find out soon enough.

Biggie decided to have Rosebud drive her out to the hospital to see how Laura was doing. After they left, I went into the kitchen to find Willie Mae and tell her all about me and Misty finding Stacie. She was rolling out a piecrust on the table, but she kept saying "Uh-huh," while I talked, so I was sure she was listening. Finally, she said, "That all?"

"I guess. Biggie knows more than she's telling. I can tell. Willie Mae, she makes me so mad when she does that. What would it hurt for her to tell me what she's thinking?"

"Reckon I knows who done it, too." She rolled the dough around her rolling pin and laid it over the pie pan.

"How? Willie Mae, how could you know? Oh . . . I forgot. . . ." What I forgot was that Willie Mae is a voodoo lady. She knows most everything. "Who?"

"You be finding out soon enough." She trimmed the extra dough from around the pie and started pricking it with a fork.

"Willie Mae, say you know, too. But how could you? You don't even know those people."

"Maybe I do, and maybe I don't."

I got up and left the room. I know when I'm licked. I went into the den and picked up the phone to call Monica, figuring she'd be interested in the latest developments.

"So that's it," I said, after I'd told her everything. "Me and Misty found that old gal and brought her home."

"Hey, that Misty, she's something, isn't she?" Monica said. "I could be friends with her."

"Yeah."

"I've got an idea, J.R. Why don't you find her a date for the dance? We could go on a double date!"

"Umm . . ." I thought fast. "I don't know . . . I'll have to think. . . ."

"Okay, you think about it. Guess what! My mom's gone and bought me a new dress. I will have to wear a dress, won't I?" I have never in my life seen Monica wearing a dress.

"Yeah, I guess."

"And something else, J.R."

"What?"

"She's bought me a wig. I tried the thing on, and it doesn't look all that bad. Now you won't have to be embarrassed or anything—taking an old girl with only half her hair to the dance."

"Hey, I wouldn't . . . but you see, the thing is . . ."

"I got to go now. Papa's got the truck stuck down by the creek. I've got to help him get it out. Bye."

I went outside and shot baskets in the driveway until Biggie and Rosebud drove up. Soon after, Willie Mae stuck her head out the door and called me to come to supper. We had King Ranch Chicken Casserole with warm homemade flour tortillas to go with it. We also had green jellied salad with cottage cheese, crushed pineapple, and grated carrots, which frankly, is not one of my favorite things, but I ate a little just to be polite. The pie was cherry, my favorite.

"So, how was Laura?" Willie Mae asked, setting my milk in front of me.

"No change." Biggie took a large helping of casserole. "Umm, this is good. The doctor says she could wake up any minute just fine, she could have brain damage, or she may never wake up."

"Never wake up?" I stopped spreading butter on my tortilla.

"That's right. They just don't know."

"The same thing happened to my cousin, Theotus Robichaux," Rosebud said. "He got kicked upside the head by a mule." He winked at Willie Mae. "That boy slept for seven days and seven nights. On the seventh day, he got up out of bed and went outside and commenced plowin' just like nothin' had ever happened."

"I don't believe that, Rosebud. He must have been hungry."

"Well, now that I recollect, I believe he did ask his wife to fry him up a mess of bacon and eggs before he left. But soon's he finished eatin' he went back to plowin'."

I giggled. "Didn't he have to go to the bathroom?"

"Hush," Biggie said, "I hear the doorbell. That must be Red Upchurch. Willie Mae, we'll have pie and coffee in the den." She went to answer the door, then took the ranger directly to the den and shut the door.

I had started up the stairs to my bedroom when the best idea of my whole life came to me in a flash. I had the solution to my problem, if only I could pull it off. I came back downstairs and, after peeking into the den and seeing Biggie and the ranger sitting on the couch, heads together, I picked up the hall telephone and dialed a number. My heart pounded as I heard the receiver being lifted on the other side of the line. When I hung up, I let out a sigh of relief and sprinted upstairs to my room.

At six-thirty, I tapped on the den door. "Biggie! *Wheel of Fortune* is coming on." That is Biggie's all-time favorite television show.

The door opened and Biggie came out followed by Ranger Upchurch. "Never mind," she said, "we're going out to the ranch. Where is Rosebud?"

I ran to get Rosebud, and quick as a chicken on a June bug, we were all piled in the car and headed for the country.

22

Someone had built a fire in the fireplace in the great room and the family was gathered around it when we walked in. Babe and Rob sat together on the sofa while Grace Higgins, wearing riding britches and boots, stood by the hearth with her elbow propped on the mantel. Abner looked uncomfortable in a straight chair he had pulled in from the dining room. Hamp lounged in a big leather club chair with his arm around Misty, who was perched beside him. Stacie, dressed in a fluffy robe and slippers, was curled up in the matching leather chair on the opposite side of the hearth. She glanced at Grace and quickly looked away again. The ranger whispered something to Biggie. She walked out to the center of the group.

"As you now know," she said, "Rex Barnwell meant a great deal to me in my youth. He didn't deserve to be shot in cold blood, and I made it my business to find his killer. I have done that." She looked around at the startled faces in the room. All but one, that is. Stacie only continued to look glum. Biggie moved over to Stacie's chair and looked down at her. "Now, young lady, I believe you have a story to tell."

Stacie looked down at her lap. "I won't," she said.

"You must," Biggie said. "You can't hurt her now."

Now she looked up at Biggie with eyes like a deer caught in the headlights. "You mean . . . ?"

"Oh, no!" Grace gasped.

The ranger spoke to Stacie. "You can talk here or at the jail. You won't like it down there."

"I'm not going to jail!" Stacie buried her face in her hands and sobbed. "You can't make me. I didn't do murder."

"But you know who did," the ranger said. "You might as well tell us. She wouldn't want you to lie anymore."

Stacie stared into the fire for a long time. Then she sighed. "Maybe you're right." She sat up straight and crossed her feet at her ankles. "But I'll have to tell you about me so you'll understand."

Biggie nodded. "Go on, honey."

Stacie took a deep breath. "The day I was born, I was a ward of the state. My birth mother was just a kid and couldn't take care of me. There was some kind of problem with letting me be adopted—something about my birth father refusing to sign away his rights." She sniffed loudly and Grace pulled a tissue out of her pocket and handed it to her. "Finally, when I was four, I was sent to a home . . . or a hellhole. It was run by a preacher and his

191

wife. Hellfire and brimstone types. Their motto was: Spare the rod and spoil the child. Well, they sure didn't spare the rod—only in our case it was rubber hoses, one for beating us and the other for spraying us with cold water when we acted up. We slept on hard mats on the floor and ate barely enough to keep us alive and able to work on the farm, where they grew organic vegetables to sell to fancy stores."

"That's horrible," Babe said.

"You don't know the half of it." Stacie frowned at her. "And you never will because you're just a spoiled brat."

For once, Babe kept her mouth shut.

"Go on," Biggie said.

"I was one of the lucky ones," she continued. "I didn't die. Some did, and they were buried under the cornfield."

"I don't believe it." Rob was shocked. "The authorities would have known."

"That's what you think," Stacie said. "The preacher, his name was Brother Jimson, and his wife were the best liars in the world. When the social workers came around, they'd just say the dead kids were off visiting friends or some such thing. The fools never caught on. That is until one official got smart. He started in questioning us kids. At first we were too scared to talk." She stopped. "I'm hungry and I'm thirsty!"

The ranger went into the kitchen and shortly Josefina came out and set down a tray with a glass of milk and a plate of cookies on the table beside Stacie. Stacie ate a whole cookie and drank half the glass of milk before she would say another word.

"So what happened next?" Biggie prodded.

192

"They closed the place, and we were all sent to other foster homes." Stacie shuddered. "I had nightmares for years about Brother Jimson coming to take me back again."

"But he never came?" Babe asked.

Stacie gave her a scornful look. "Of course not. He was in jail. Then I went to live with a family in Waco. They had a bunch of us kids, as many as five at one time. They paid their bills by taking in foster kids. But they fed us good and gave us a clean place to sleep. We all used to wonder about our birth families. In bed at night, we'd talk about finding them someday. Naturally, we all imagined our real parents had been searching for us all our lives—and they were all rich."

"But your dream came true." Biggie said.

"Uh-huh."

"Tell us about that."

"It was just a miracle, that's all. See, what happened, I had been starved so much as a little kid that when I got enough to eat, I just couldn't stop. I got fatter and fatter until the doctor told my foster parents something had to be done. I was getting what he called 'morbidly obese.' He told my foster mother about this place, and I was sent here. The miracle was, my very own mother was the owner."

"Laura." Biggie said.

"Yeah. I'd been pretty miserable here from the very first and showed it. She"—she pointed to Grace—"reminded me of old Brother Jimson, the way she treated us mean and made us work."

"It was for your own good," Grace said.

193

"Yeah, that's what he said, too. But then one day Laura took me aside and told me she had found out from my birth records that she was my own long-lost mother. She said she'd been searching for me ever since the day she gave me away. I was the happiest kid alive."

"Well, you sure didn't act that way." Misty spoke for the first time.

"I know. Laura told me to act the same as I always had—that we couldn't tell anyone about us. It was our secret, you see."

"Why?" Babe wanted to know.

"Because she thought the others might resent me if they knew."

"Hogwash," Abner grunted.

"I agree," said Grace. "You should have told us all."

"Well, that wasn't all," Stacie continued. "See, Laura had a problem. The camp was costing a lot more than she thought it would. Since old Rex had gotten sick, she had been taking money out of his investment accounts. I guess that lawyer found out and told Rex about it. Anyway, she was afraid he would, so she said we had to help Rex out of his misery; then she could inherit his money and she'd be able to keep helping poor overweight girls like me. She loved us all." Stacie looked around the room. "All she ever wanted to do was help people."

Babe stood up. "Are you telling us you murdered my daddy? I ought to kill you now!"

The ranger stepped forward and put his hand on Babe's shoulder. She glared at him but sat back down.

"How was it done?" Biggie's voice was calm, but her eyes flashed.

Stacie sighed. "I don't guess it matters now. The only person I ever loved is dead."

"So what happened." Abner's voice was grim.

"Remember the night he died? How I came in acting crazy, and took Laura into the study?"

"Of course we remember," Babe said. "Get on with it!"

"We had it all planned. As soon as we got in there, Laura took the gun and slipped out the French doors. I followed to watch. She hurried across the patio and shot Rex through the window. She missed the first time and hit Jeremy. The second shot killed Rex. Then the gun accidentally went off again. She was really nervous. After she flipped the breaker switch so the lights would go out she came back into the study where you found us both." She looked smugly around at the group. "You'd have never figured it out, if I hadn't told you."

"I'm afraid you're wrong, young lady," the ranger said. "We were damn close to figuring it out. You've just filled in some of the blanks."

Just then, the phone rang. Grace went into the hall to answer it. When she came back in, she had a look on her face that was a mixture of relief and something else—fear, I guess. She sat down quickly on the couch as if she might fall if she didn't. "Laura's awake," she said. "And she's okay!"

Stacie leaped out of her chair faster than a mountain lion and jumped on top of Biggie. Growling like an animal, she put her hands around Biggie's throat and began to choke her. "You lied!" she screamed and tightened her grip.

The rest of sat openmouthed while Ranger Upchurch and Rosebud pulled Stacie away. She fought like a sack of wildcats, but the two of them finally got her subdued and back in her chair. My heart was in my throat as I went to Biggie.

Later at home, we sat around the fire in the den. Biggie, curled up in her chair and drinking a hot herbal drink Willie Mae had made to soothe her throat, spoke first. "For the first time in my life, I reckon I've looked pure evil in the face."

"Stacie?" I asked.

"No, honey, that girl was just a pawn. Laura."

" 'For the lips of the strange woman drop as an honeycomb, and her mouth is smoother than oil, but her end is bitter as wormwood, sharp as a two-edged sword. Her feet go down to death; her steps take hold on hell.' " Willie Mae spoke in a funny singsong voice.

"Huh?" I said.

"Exactly," Biggie said. "It's from the Bible, honey."

Rosebud stood up to throw another log on the fire. "What's gonna happen now?"

"A long recovery, I'm sure," Biggie said. "Then Red Upchurch intends to make sure Laura goes on trial for first-degree murder."

"Why did she have to kill him? I'd just found my new granddaddy, and she had to go and do that before I even got to know him. He was about to die anyway." The more I thought about it, the madder I got.

"She had to move fast. Jeremy Polk had begun to sense something was wrong. I imagine he had already

196

confided his suspicions to Rex. Then, too, I think she was hoping she'd get the job done before he had a chance to change his will."

"What's gonna happen to Stacie and the rest of them girls?" Willie Mae asked.

"Most of them will just go back home, I guess," Biggie said. "As for Stacie, she's almost sixteen. I suppose she could go back into foster care. Of course, there's the possibility she may be sent to juvenile detention. I doubt it, though. It's pretty obvious she was used and manipulated by Laura. What she needs most is psychiatric care. I'll just have to talk to the judge about that."

"Why would you want to do that, Biggie? She tried to kill you."

"Well, I . . ."

Rosebud broke in. "That little gal's had a hard row to hoe. I reckon she could use a friend. . . ."

"That's exactly right, Rosebud. Tomorrow I'll go down and talk to Judge Bass about it."

"Was she really Laura's daughter?" I asked.

Biggie's face hardened. "Not for a minute. Laura only made up that story to trick Stacie into doing what she wanted. The baby bracelet we found? That belonged to Babe. Laura hung on to it because she thought it might be useful—and maybe to keep it out of Babe's hands."

"That's really cold," I said.

"You right about that." Rosebud stretched his feet out so they'd be closer to the fire. "How'd you figure out how they done it, Miss Biggie?"

"I didn't know for sure. But when J.R. told me he'd seen the curtain blowing in that study on the night of the murder, then later the door was sealed and plants were growing just outside, well that started me thinking. . . ." Biggie yawned and stretched. "Any more questions?"

We all shook our heads.

"Good." She set her mug down and stood up. "I'm off to bed then."

The others followed, but I stayed in the den watching the fire until it died down. Then I went to the hall phone and called Misty. I had something to say to her that couldn't wait until tomorrow.

Two Weeks Later

When I came home from the dance, everyone was sitting around the kitchen table drinking coffee and waiting. I had taken off the sport coat and tie Biggie had made me wear. Now I tossed them onto a chair and went to the refrigerator to pour myself a glass of milk. I took a seat at the table to drink it, feeling three pairs of eyes, two brown and one blue, boring into me.

"What?" I asked.

"How was it?" Rosebud asked.

"It was okay."

"Well, did you have a good time?" This was Biggie.

"I guess. Are there any cookies left?"

Willie Mae went to the pantry and set a bag of store-bought cookies in front of me. "Did you dance?"

"Uh-huh."

"Who'd you dance with?" Biggie wanted to know.

I took a bite off an Oreo and took a swig of milk. "Lots of people."

"Name one." Biggie was getting exasperated.

"Misty, mostly." I sighed.

"Were they all surprised when you come walkin' in with two gals on your arm?" This was Rosebud.

I sighed. I figured if I was ever going to get to bed, I'd better come clean. "Yeah. Their eyes just about popped outta their heads when we walked in the door. The funny thing was, Monica didn't even look like herself. With that new dress and her wig, she was a fox. The guys all wanted to dance with her, so I was stuck with Misty most of the night. Once when I tried to cut in on DeWayne Boggs while he was dancing a slow dance with old Monica, he threatened to punch me out. Who would of believed it?"

"Who indeed?" Biggie said.

I stood up. "Can I go to bed now? I'm supposed to go out to the farm tomorrow. Me and Monica are going persimmon picking."

Willie Mae's
King Ranch Casserole

There are many versions of the famous King Ranch Casserole in Texas, but we think Willie Mae's is the best.

1	can cream of chicken soup	1	bag Doritos brand corn chips
1	can cream of mushroom soup	1	(3 or 4 pound) chicken, boiled
1	pint sour cream	1	cup broth from chicken
1	(10 ounce) can Rotel Tomatoes and Green Chiles	2	cups grated Monterey Jack cheese

Boil your chicken good until the meat is falling off the bones. Let it cool. Oil up a casserole dish. I use about a three-quart one. Then you mix up your soups and your sour cream with enough chicken broth to make it about as thick as good creamy gravy. Put some corn chips in the bottom of the dish, then put in half the chicken, which you have pulled off the bone and cut in pieces. Next you pour on half the soup mixture. Do that again then sprinkle on your cheese. Bake at 350 degrees for about an hour—or less if it gets done sooner.

Serve this up with a good salad. I like Bibb lettuce with avocado slices, dressed with a little lime juice and olive oil.